My Billionaire Fake Husband

BLAIRE W. KINSLEY

Copyright © 2023 by Blaire W. Kinsley

All rights reserved.

No part of this book may be reproduced in any form or by any electronic or mechanical means, including information storage and retrieval systems, without written permission from the author, except for the use of brief quotations in a book review.

CHAPTER 1
Michelle

The little voice in my head is telling me that opening up my electric bill is a bad idea; today is one of my very few days off, and this could tank all the efforts I've put into relaxing today. Still, I use my long, black fingernails to rip into the envelope to pull out the statement.

I read it once, then twice, because I'm sure I must be misreading it. "Why is this $164?!" I ask my empty living room.

I think I can count on my hands the number of full days I spent here last month. Mostly, I use this place to sleep, shower, and do laundry, so the number in front of me shouldn't be so surprising. But last month, it was hot, and I kept my apartment cold. So, this is on me for keeping the AC running when I'm not home.

I groan and toss the bill onto my coffee table, where it blends in with the rest of the clutter I've accumulated. Earlier today, I told myself I'd clean up, but I'm not so sure I have the energy to do that anymore. Anxiety over money is eating me alive, and I think I might just spend the rest of the day sitting here, staring at the mess.

Lately, I've been wondering if my apartment is really worth it. When I moved in, this place was a deal; I collected a hefty signing special, and it was right before rent in the city started skyrocketing. I only renewed my lease because they were offering a free month of rent if I accepted their renewal offer early.

Since then, I've struggled to make ends meet every month. It's not for lack of trying either; I work at the breakfast place around the corner three days at the beginning of the week, and then most nights, I'm a bottle girl at Metro, a club only a couple blocks away from here.

This is my first day off in a while, although now I wish it wasn't.

Paying that electric bill is going to be a bitch. I don't even want to think about my internet and phone payment dates that are coming up. God, it feels like I just paid rent, but that's right around the corner again, too.

I wonder if my mom would let me move back home; she turned my old bedroom into her office, but I could convince her to part with the space. Probably.

My phone ringing on the kitchen counter pulls me out of my thoughts. Letting it go to voicemail crosses my mind, but curiosity gets the best of me like it always does, and I hurry to see who's calling. It's Jake, my boss at the nightclub.

"Hello?" I say, unlocking and answering the phone before it's fully against my ear.

"Michelle, hey," Jake says, sounding like he doesn't want to have this conversation. "How's your day off going?"

"It's fine," I reply, suspicious of his tone; he's either firing me or asking me to cover a shift. I'm hoping for the latter. "What's up?"

"Oh, nothing, I was just calling to ask something, and you

can say no, by the way. No pressure or anything," he says, and I really wish he'd just be forward with this. "It's just that Alyssa called off, and we're already understaffed as it is–"

"Do you want me to come in tonight?" I ask, cutting him off. He and Miles both know I want more hours but always seem hesitant to ask me to pick them up.

"Yes," he says, sounding relieved that I've said it for him. "Like I said, you don't have to. I know you work all the time."

"I'll come in," I say quickly, unwilling to listen to his platitudes. "What time do you want me?"

"Nine. Alyssa was supposed to close, but we're not going to make you do that," he says. "We really appreciate this."

"No problem," I say, resisting the urge to tell him how much this means to *me*. "I'll see you tonight."

"That you will," he replies, sounding a lot lighter than when we started this phone call. Bye, Michelle."

"Bye, Jake," I say, hanging up and dropping my phone back on the counter.

I waste no time getting into the shower — my legs need to be shaved desperately, my armpits, too, if I'm being honest with myself.

I take my time, making sure I don't miss any spots, even taking the time to exfoliate. I'm sitting on the edge of the tub, massaging lotion into my calf, when my phone starts going off in the other room again.

"Dammit," I say, standing and wiping the excess lotion from my hands onto my stomach before snatching my towel from the rack and pulling it tightly around my body.

The ringing stops as soon as I get into the kitchen. One missed FaceTime call from Pippa, my childhood best friend, is displayed brightly on the screen. I don't think we've ever gone more than a few days without talking to each other; she rarely lets us go for more than a few hours.

I call her back and carry my phone back into the bathroom so I can finish moisturizing myself and get a head start on putting on my face.

"It's your day off," Pippa says when she appears on the screen. "Why didn't you answer me? Do you have a hot date or something?"

"Hi, Pippa," I say, propping her up against the mirror. "You're right, it is my day off, but I picked up a shift."

"You're going to work yourself to death," she replies, the door to her office closing with a decisive click on the other end. "I'm starting to worry about you."

"Someone has to pay rent," I say lightly; it's not that I don't want to share my struggles with her, but I need to be in a better mood when I get to work tonight. "What's up?"

"Works been hell," she grumbles, bringing her baby blue vape up to her mouth and leaving wine-red lipstick on the device. "We have six more HVAC units out on this property today."

Thick white vapor swirls around her head, the wind whipping it and her blonde hair around wildly. She hits her vape again.

"And the residents are pissed. Rightfully so, but still," she groans. "Sometimes I really hate my job."

"You don't mean that," I reply as I rub the last of the lotion into my thigh and move onto my arms; Pippa's worked her way up the ladder in property management and has three apartment communities under her jurisdiction. "What about your place?"

"I said *sometimes*," she replies before looking closely at the screen. "Why are you naked?"

"I told you I picked up a shift tonight," I say, rolling my eyes. "I just got out of the shower."

"I'm being so serious, Chelle; you need a vacation."

"I *know*," I reply, stepping away from the camera to grab my makeup. When I come back into the frame, I say, "Trust me, Pips, you're preaching to the choir with that one."

"You should visit me," she offers; it's not even the first time she's brought it up this week. "Your bedroom misses you."

"Oh, whatever," I say, patting foundation onto my face. "The bedroom doesn't miss me."

"You're right," she concedes. "I miss you."

"You talk to me every day," I remind her. "Technically, you see me every day, too."

"But I can't touch you," she whines, dramatically leaning against the wall of her building.

"Yeah, that's not totally weird," I mumble, starting on a smokey eye that'll make my brown eyes look a little more golden in the club lighting.

"You know what I mean," she shoots back, her laughter muffled by the wild wind. "I miss hanging out with you, dude. It's impossible to get you to take any time off work."

I sigh, electing to continue on my eye makeup while I try to figure out how to tell her I'm completely fucked financially without making my situation seem as bleak as it is. Thankfully, she doesn't seem to notice I'm stalling; she's currently busy trying to tame her hair.

"Whatever you make on a good night at Metro, I'll double it if you come hang out with me," Pippa offers, giving up on her hair and letting the wind take it. "Dead serious."

"Have you ever considered that I like my job?" I ask. Taking Pippa's help has always been out of the question, even though she definitely has enough money to spare. I grab my eyeliner and start putting it on, adding, "I'm also definitely not comfortable asking you to give me *that* much money."

"You're not asking," she says casually. "I'm offering."

"Let me think about it," I say, knowing I'm not going to think about it at all.

"Sure," she says, hitting her vape one more time before pushing away from the wall. "I have to get back in there. I left the new hire to man the office alone."

"That sounds like it was a good idea," I say sarcastically. "I'm sure the angry residents took it easy on her."

"Look, I know this sounds harsh, but this is just how property management is," she says, pushing the door open. "This isn't her first rodeo."

"I believe you."

"Whatever, asshole," she teases. "I have to go. Think about visiting me, okay?"

"I will," I lie, capping my eyeliner. "I love you. I hope the rest of your day is easy."

"That's doubtful. Love you, too, babe."

Pippa isn't even looking at her phone when she hangs up; there was probably an angry resident on their way to the office to complain. For all of the perks of her job, I can't say I envy her. She's responsible for people's homes; tempers get high fast.

I might be stressed about money, but at least work's fun. Sure, a customer gets belligerent every once in a while, but usually, it's more entertaining than anything else. Plus, I have the power to kick them out; it's not like Pippa can kick someone out of their house for being an asshole.

When I pull the towel away from my hair, I shake out my dark brown waves, and they fall over my shoulders, covering my breasts. I've been thinking about cutting it. I don't mind the length, but if it gets any longer styling it is going to be a real pain in the ass. As it is, all I have to do is work some mousse through it, and it looks like I actually made an effort. I value my time.

I do pull my curling iron out, though. I've still got a few hours before I have to think about getting to the club, and I'm trying to make as much money as I can tonight. Unfortunately, that electric bill isn't going to pay itself.

CHAPTER 2
Tom

"You're *such* a fucking idiot," Victor says through full-body laughter; he's shaking so hard the amber liquid in his glass threatens to slosh onto the table.

"Just because you're not on the clock doesn't mean I'm not still your boss," I warn good-naturedly. Truthfully, I deserve the ribbing.

"When Ryan finds out you lied, I doubt you're going to be heading this team," he shoots back.

I run a hand over my face as my team breaks out into laughter that I know is on the wrong side of good-natured. I wait for their laughter to be overtaken by the music pumping through the club before loudly declaring, "I don't know why you'd joke like that. If I'm out, so are all of you."

"We're just having a good time," Eddy promises, grabbing the bottle of whiskey from the center of the table and dumping the last of it into my glass. "I'm sure he'll totally understand that you were lying about having a wife."

"Yeah, Tom," Victor says, jabbing me with his elbow. "Just tell him you were saying whatever you could to get his money. You weren't expecting him to want to meet her, that's all. It's a simple misunderstanding, really."

"You know, I'm sure he'll still want to go through with the deal," Eddy continues, feeding off of Victor's chaotic energy. "Lying about having a wife is exactly what a family man would do. He's going to trust you with his app. For sure."

Before anyone can say anything else, our waitress appears at the head of the table to save me. Her name is Michelle, and she's been taking care of me and these bozos on my team for the last six months. It started by chance; my table just happened to be in her section a couple of times in a row. After that, I started requesting her when she was at work, which is pretty much all the time.

"Are we behaving over here?" she asks, her manicured hand resting on her hip and an eyebrow quirked in Eddy's direction like she suspects he's the one who started it.

"Yes, ma'am," he says, feigning an innocent smile at her; if I weren't trying to behave, I'd slap him for being so facetious. "We're always on our best behavior for you."

Michelle is completely unimpressed by his antics and directs her attention toward me. I think she's waiting for an explanation, but I'd rather she didn't know how much of a fucking idiot I am so my mouth stays shut tight. When she realizes I'm not talking, she looks at Victor.

"Guess what Tom did," he says, delighted to be the center of her attention; apparently, all of my guys have crushes on her. I can't say I blame them.

She drags her eyes back to me and says, "Well. What did you do?"

"He told our new client he's *married*," Victor continues, and I can't help but think his glee might be contagious if it weren't at my expense.

"Our *potential* new client," Eddy corrects him before looking back at me apathetically. "Although, we're probably not going to close on that deal when they find out Tommy boy here is a big, fat liar."

"Would you stop?" I ask, thankful for the darkness of the club; I can feel my face getting hot, and I can't bring myself to look at anyone, opting to stare at my overfull glass instead.

Horribly, Michelle laughs. It's a sweet sound, not harsh or derisive. Still, it stings way more than the teasing from the guys.

"You're kidding, right?" she asks, running a hand through her perfectly curled hair. "Please tell me they're kidding, Tom. You're smarter than this."

"Apparently, I'm not," I say, finally speaking. "They're not kidding."

"No," she says, sounding scandalized and glancing at the others to gauge for signs of lying. "How did this happen?"

I hold up a finger and swallow two gulps of my drink before saying, "I may have gotten carried away at a networking event."

"You got so carried away you made up a wife you don't have?" she asks incredulously, and when I risk looking at her, there's a look that falls somewhere between disbelief and amusement. "How?"

"Alcohol may have been involved," I admit. "A lot of it."

"Clearly."

"He asked if I was a family man, and I said yes," I reply, shrugging. "Then he asked if I was married."

"And you said yes?" she asks, cracking up when I nod my head sadly. "Did he not notice you weren't wearing a ring?"

"I kept my left hand in my pocket the rest of the night," I say. "It was miserable."

"Sounds like you did it to yourself," she laughs, glancing

at another one of her tables. "I've got to run and check on my other tables. Can I grab y'all anything while I'm gone? Looks like you're outta whiskey."

"We're good, but if you find someone stupid enough to marry Tom on short notice, send her our way," Victor says.

"No offense," Michelle says, sugary sweet, "but you can't leave me a tip big enough for me to play matchmaker."

With that, she struts off, leaving us to watch her retreat. Her hips sway effortlessly, and her legs are toned and shapely, her heels making them look impossibly long. My eyes linger on her ass for longer than totally necessary.

"So," Eddy starts, breaking us out of our trance, his voice strangely loud over the bass in the speakers, "what are you going to do?"

"I have no idea," I say, my head starting to feel fuzzy from all the alcohol I've had in the last few hours. "I need a wife. Badly."

"Tell him she's sick and couldn't make it," he suggests earnestly. "Not like that's something you can control."

"He'd see right through me," I groan, pinching my brow. "Plus, I don't think he'll trust FamFirst, an app that's supposed to help families find nannies and family-friendly events, to someone that doesn't have a family."

"Is a wife *really* a family?" Victor asks, unnecessarily skeptical. "Don't you need kids for that?"

"A wife is a family," I say sharply in defense of my hypothetical wife. "What are you even saying, man?"

"A wife means the prospect of a family," Eddy says, trying to find a middle ground and get us back on track. He throws back the rest of his drink and pushes the glass away with his fingertip. "We'll find you a wife. When do you need her by again?"

"We can't just *find* a wife," I argue. "Plus, their little

meeting thing is this weekend. That's not a lot of time to find someone."

"That's three days. We can definitely find you, someone," Victor says, slamming his hand on the table to punctuate his point. "We can start looking now."

"No way," I say, horrified at the idea of asking any of these women to marry me for a business deal. "Let's just admit it, boys. I'm fucked."

"What about an escort?" Eddy asks, sending Victor into a fit of hysterics.

His laughter gets to me, and I can barely get out, "I'm not bringing a *call girl* to a business meeting. There's no way I'd be able to pass her off as my wife."

"You're so right," Victor says when he gets himself under control, a joyful lilt still in his voice. "You need someone you have *chemistry* with."

"Too bad you don't have chemistry with a single woman we know," Eddy laments.

I resist the urge to throttle him right here at the table in front of God and everyone. Instead, I take a slow, calculated sip while maintaining eye contact with him in an attempt to assert some sort of dominance. Unfortunately, this situation just keeps spiraling further and further out of my control.

"Maybe we could ask Michelle," Victor says, his eyes scanning the crowd in search of her. "You guys get along well enough."

"We only get along because I'm paying her," I say, pointing out the obvious.

"Dude!" Eddy cries, snapping his fingers like we've cracked some sort of secret code. "That's it!"

"What's it?" I ask, unsure of whether or not I actually want to hear his answer.

"Pay Michelle to be your fake wife," he says, apparently annoyed I didn't pick up on the obvious.

"She has a job," I point out, eager for an excuse *not* to ask her to play my wife for money. "She's probably working this weekend."

Victor rolls his eyes. "Offer her more money than she'd make here, then."

"I–" I start to protest, but Eddy's caught Michelle's attention, and she's weaving through the crowd to get back to our table.

"You guys decide you wanted another bottle after all?" she asks when she stops at the end of our table.

"We do, actually," Eddy says; he's overly confident, and I wish I could disappear. "But first, I have kind of a personal question."

"Sure," she says, resting her hand on her hip, "but you know I won't hesitate to throw you out if you say something out of line. So tread lightly."

"Well, we have a business opportunity for you," he says, his best professional voice not covering up the fact that he's very close to being drunk. "I need to know how much money you stand to make here this weekend, though."

God, he sounds so creepy.

"Uh," she starts, not expecting the question, "if everyone tips well, and they better, close to a grand."

"What if I told you that you could make two thousand dollars if you help us out this weekend instead," Eddy says.

She looks away from him and fixes me with a look that screams *help me,* but I'm not sure I know how to help. Honestly, my brain's kind of stuck on Eddy offering two thousand of *my* dollars, because there's no way this is something I can expense, to Michelle.

"If I said yes," she says, turning back to Eddy when I don't give her what she wants, "what do I have to do?"

"Oh, nothing really," he says casually. "You'll just have to ride to Houston with Tom and pretend to be his wife for the night on Friday."

Her eyes are on me again, and I can tell she *also* has no idea what to make of this. "Is this your solution to the mess you've made?"

"It's not my solution," I say weakly, glancing at Victor and Eddy. "But I hate to admit that it's probably the best one we have right now."

"Oh, wow," she mutters so quietly I read her lips more than I hear her. "Two grand? Seriously?"

"Yeah," I say, committing to the number. I can swing it, and if we can get Ryan on board, I'll make way more than that back.

Her nails click against the table as she considers the offer. Finally, she says, "Let me think about it. I'll have to talk to Jake first. I don't know if this place can afford me being gone this weekend."

She's about to walk away when the meaning of her words actually catches up with me.

"Wait," I say, my alcohol-soaked brain moving infuriatingly slowly. "Is that a yes?"

"It's a yes only if my boss says I can go."

CHAPTER 3
Michelle

"You know, Michelle," Pippa begins, taking a loud bite of her absurdly large salad, "this might be the single stupidest, most dangerous thing you've ever done."

I look away from the mess of clothes on my bed, giving her my full attention when I say, "You've said that four times, babe."

"I just wanted to make sure you heard me," she says through a mouthful of vegetables. "Because this is dangerous and stupid."

"Tom's been coming into the club for almost a year," I tell her, grabbing the dress I plan on wearing to the dinner I'm on the hook for tomorrow night. "He's been *my* regular for more than six months. I'm going to be fine."

"How can you be so sure?" she asks, and I don't have to look at her to know she has her eyes narrowed and her nose scrunched. "Really?"

"Jake thinks I'll be fine."

"Why are you taking safety advice from men?" she asks. "Come on; you're smarter than this."

I'm not sure how to tell Pippa I'm only doing this because the money he's offering me is too good to turn down. If she knew the whole truth, she'd insist on sending me more than that to keep me home.

I feel a lot more comfortable taking Tom's money than I do taking hers.

"I know my way around Houston. You have my location," I say instead, glancing toward her again. "And you're in the area. So I'll be okay."

"You've still got a two-hour drive with that guy," she reminds me. "Anything could happen."

"Pips," I say, pausing my packing efforts. It's sweet that she's so concerned about me, actually, even if it's totally unwarranted. "I'll be okay. I need you to trust me on this one."

"You're not the one I don't trust."

"Tom needs me to help him close this deal," I say, throwing three pairs of panties into my bag; I definitely won't need them, but overpacking underwear is a habit I'm never going to break. "That's all this is. I know you don't believe this, but Jake wouldn't let me go anywhere with this guy if he thought I wasn't going to be safe."

"I think you need to be more skeptical of men in general, Pippa posits.

"Your hatred of men was cute when we were in college," I reply, zipping my suitcase with a flourish, "but now it's kind of exhausting. Who hurt you?"

"Men! So many men!" she yells, stabbing the air with her fork. "I thought that was obvious."

I laugh and shake my head, picking my phone up from where it's propped up against some pillows.

"It was," I say, unable to stop myself from chuckling at her antics. "I guess I shouldn't have asked a stupid question."

"There are no stupid questions," she says sagely.

"You know that's not true," I chuckle, flopping down on my couch and throwing my feet onto the coffee table. "There are *plenty* of stupid questions."

"You rarely ask them, though," Pippa says, shoving another forkful of lettuce into her mouth. She swallows the overly large bite and asks, "Are you going to see me while you're here?"

"I'm going to try," I promise. "I'm not really sure what our itinerary looks like."

"Fancy word," she grins. "Even if you can't make time, I'll just show up wherever you are and crash the party. I'm not afraid."

"I'm literally begging you not to do that," I say, knowing she's mostly serious. "Tom's trying to close on this deal."

"Oh, whatever," she pouts. "You're no fun; you know that?"

"I'm plenty of fun," I reply, nonplussed by the dig. "I just know how to behave in a professional setting."

Pippa makes an exaggerated gagging noise before saying, "I have to go; you're making me sick. I don't even know who you are anymore."

"Don't say that," I laugh, shaking my head at her. "You're just mad I'm not listening to you."

"You're damn right I'm mad," she says. "I think you're doing something *very* stupid."

I just smirk at her; there's no reason to feed into this argument. She's not changing my mind, and I'm not changing hers.

"I'll see you this weekend," I say kindly. "I'll let you get back to your salad."

"You know, this salad would never hurt me the way you're hurting me."

"Bye, Pippa," I say, hanging up and tossing my cell phone aside.

As my head falls against the back of the couch, I have to admit to myself that Pippa is right. I probably shouldn't be going somewhere with a man I only know as a customer, but the money's too good to turn down. Doing this might actually allow me to put something in my savings account this month. Maybe it'll make a difference.

I glance at the electric bill that hasn't quite gotten lost in the noise of my coffee table yet. Maybe I'd be better off switching to paperless statements; at least then, I wouldn't have evidence of all the money I owe everyone lying around.

Against my better judgment once again, I pluck it from its place among the clutter and stare at the number again. It hasn't changed or magically gone away in the last two days, nor did I misread it like I was hoping. The number is still twice as high as it normally is.

I try to parse through the usage breakdown, but it doesn't make any sense to me. So I toss it back on the table and pick up my credit card bill, but that's even more bothersome. It's close to maxed out *and* was due four days ago.

Shit. Shit, shit, shit.

I'm on my phone again in an instant, logging into my account and making the minimum payment. Thank god I'm not planning on buying a house anytime soon; my credit is a mess and just keeps taking hits due to my own incompetence.

I feel like I can't get a handle on *anything* in my life. Apparently, I can't even remember to pay my bills. They're due on the same day every month. If I could put them on autopay, I would, but doing that would put my bank account at risk of being overdrawn.

When I finish checking to make sure I didn't miss another payment somewhere in the shuffle, I put my elbows on my knees and rest my head in my hands. I'm twenty-seven years old; surely, I should have outgrown this by now.

Although, maybe I should have expected this. My earliest memory is of when I was five; my mom took me to the park, and we had a competition to see who could find the most plastic and aluminum bottles. She let me win, and then we took them to the recycling center. Mom used that money to buy me my first McDonald's Happy Meal. These were such a rare treat that I didn't get another one until I was seven.

Mom and I are both way better off now, but I have *got* to be more careful. It's easy to lose everything; my mom didn't let me forget that.

I blink hard, hating that tears are starting to gather along my lower lash line. They don't go away, though, so I scrub at them with the back of my hand, my mascara smudging. Cursing under my breath, I go into my bathroom.

My reflection is lackluster; just a stressed girl that's about to break under the weight of her responsibilities. Nothing special, really. Same old, same old.

Getting the makeup off requires more scrubbing than is good for my skin. When I put down my overly-expensive microfiber cloth, my eyelids feel raw. I reach for my moisturizer, scooping out the last of it and dabbing it onto my cheeks and forehead.

"God," I mutter to myself, sinking onto the closed toilet lid, my eyes locked on the empty jar. "How am I *already* out of that?"

The tears are coming back. This time I don't resist the crying session that's coming on. I've been holding it together, sucking it up, for so long that I've more than earned this. I'm tired and overworked, in utter need of a break without the ability to take one.

A wave of helplessness crashes over me, and I feel like

I'm drowning in it. What happens when I burn through the extra money I make this weekend? I'm so behind that it's not like it makes a real difference. I'll put it toward credit cards and run them back up immediately. This is a trap that I'm never going to get out of.

Big, wet tears fall onto my lap, leaving dark circles on my jeans. I sniffle, and it sounds loud and pathetic in the acoustics of the bathroom. I feel so small like I need someone to swoop in and save me.

I let myself wallow in this feeling for what feels like hours before I rip off a few squares of toilet paper to blow my nose. I cringe at the noise, like the world's worst trumpet, before tossing the used tissue into the wastebasket.

I'm not sure if it's because I think it'll help me feel better or because it's a force of habit, but I end up on the couch, an episode of *Supernatural* playing on my TV. I don't have to pay attention; I've seen every episode more times than I can count.

Dean's grumbling something about a curse when my phone starts ringing. It's a number I don't have saved. I'm about to send it to voicemail, but I remember I gave Tom my number earlier. So I take a chance, praying it's him, as I unlock my phone.

"Hello?"

"Hey, Michelle? It's Tom."

"Oh, thank god," I laugh. "I was worried I answered a spam call."

"Nope, just me," he promises. "Sorry to bother you; I know it's getting late. I just wanted to see how you wanted me to send that money over. I wanted to go ahead and get it out of the way."

"Oh, uh," I start, my brain suddenly drawing a blank.

"I was just going to put your phone number into Venmo,

but I figured I should probably check with you since I'm sending so much," Tom continues casually. "I've got pretty much every money transferring app, so whatever works best for you."

"Right," I say, clearing my throat. "Venmo's fine."

"Just your phone number?"

"Yep," I confirm, feeling a little like I'm operating my body from a separate room. "Just my phone number."

"Awesome," he says. "I'm going to hop off of here and get that over to you."

"Yeah. Cool," I reply.

"I'll see you tomorrow. Does two still work for you?"

"Two's great."

"Alright. Bye, Michelle. Thanks again."

The line goes dead before I can reply. Then, five minutes later, I get a notification – a $2000 payment from Thomas Bridges.

It feels too good to be true, so I open the app. Sure enough, the money's right there. If I wanted to, I could pay my electric bill. Actually, that's exactly what I do, navigating to Austin Energy's online portal. When I finally get to the screen thanking me for my payment, it's like I can breathe again.

Then, I look at the balance in my Venmo account again. I'll transfer it over to my bank account soon, in the next ten minutes, but I can't help but *stare*. Two weekends' worth of work, right there. Most of my rent, right there.

An almost hysterical laugh bubbles out of me. I feel lighter, almost childlike, and I know at that moment that money *does* buy happiness.

CHAPTER 4
Tom

"You listen to old man music," Michelle complains with a smile on her face as she skips another song.

"You could change the playlist," I suggest, deciding to finally give her a hint; she's been struggling to find a song for long enough. "There'd be less 80s music on a playlist that isn't made up of 80s music."

"Dude," she groans, letting her head drop against the back of her seat. "You could have told me it was a problem with the playlist. I've been bitching for the last twenty minutes."

"It was kind of funny," I say instead of offering a real explanation. Then, I add, "I also assumed you'd realize it was a playlist."

"I always play stuff directly from my liked songs. I figured you did the same."

I don't answer; some pop song fills the cab of my car. I'm fairly certain I've heard it at the club before. It sounds like it's something from the Top 40. Michelle adjusts the volume of the radio, the cubic zirconia of her prop wedding ring sparking, before returning my phone to its mount; the GPS says we've only got half an hour left on the road.

"So," she says over the dull thrum of music, adjusting the hair lying on her shoulders, "what do I need to know about this stuff?"

"Honestly, nothing," I admit. "I've got all the business stuff covered. Company's called FamFirst. The founder and CEO is named Ryan. He's a good guy."

"He's the one you lied to, right?" she asks, straight to the point and without a trace of judgment.

"He would be the one," I confirm. "I'm pretty sure he's bringing his wife, too. You guys can make friends."

She laughs and shifts back in her seat. "You're already in character, I see."

"What do you mean?" I ask, glancing at her out of the corner of my eye.

"Nothing," Michelle replies, waving her hand dismissively. She picks at a rip on her jeans. "I'm not sure I understand what I have to do. This all seems too easy."

"This isn't some secret mission or anything," I say, unable to keep the laughter out of my voice. "You just have to tell people you're my wife."

"That's it?" she asks. "Nothing else?"

"Well, you have to make it convincing. They have to think you like me."

"Shit, Tom. I don't know if I can do that," she says, somehow keeping her voice completely serious. "We might have a problem."

"I wish you would have told me that before I sent you that money," I say, playing along with this little game.

"You won't be getting that back, by the way."

"I knew I should have had legal draw up a contract before I paid you," I reply without any heat, enjoying goofing around with her.

"Ah," she says like it's some kind of gotcha, "but you didn't."

I flex my hands on the steering wheel, my fake wedding band glinting in the sunlight; I can't remember the last time I had this much fun on a road trip with someone. We fall into companionable silence, Michelle's music providing a soundtrack while traffic starts to thicken as we get closer to Houston.

It takes us longer than thirty minutes to finish the trip; we get caught in an early rush hour; apparently, almost everyone in Houston got off work before five today. Strangely enough, I don't really care.

Michelle and I are engaged in an intense game of I Spy when I can finally get off the highway. The GPS struggles to locate us; the overpasses and slow crawl of my car are too much for the device to process.

"Where did you say we were going again?" she asks, scooting forward in her seat to scope out our surroundings.

"Marriott Marquis," I mutter, more focused on the cars around us than the landmarks.

"Well, we're nowhere near that."

"You know the area?"

I see her shrug out of the corner of my eye; her eyes are still focused on the streets when she says, "My best friend lives here."

"You didn't tell me that. We could try to meet up with her," I offer.

"Would you be mad at me if I told you I was already planning on doing that?" Michelle asks; I can hear the slight smile in her voice.

"Is that your way of saying you're planning on ditching me?" I tease.

"Turn here," she mutters, pointing at a side street without

much traffic. When I take the turn, she continues, "Ditching you wasn't in the plan *exactly*."

"But it was probably going to happen anyway."

"Sorry," she says, not sounding sorry at all as she turns off the navigation. "I can get us there; you're going to want to turn left when you can. And you're welcome to come with me tonight. I just figured you wouldn't want to."

"No, it's okay," I promise her, throwing on my turn signal. "Take your time with your friend. I'll probably turn in early, anyway. It's been a long week."

"You're telling me," she laughs, and I suspect she's probably had a harder week than I have.

Michelle gets us to our hotel using side streets and alleys; I'm not completely sure I didn't break a few laws, but I stop caring when I park in front of the valet station. I hand my keys off as Michelle grabs her bag and mine from the backseat, and I walk around the back of my car to join her.

"I've always wondered what the inside of this place looks like," she says, staring through the doors into the hotel lobby. "I got drinks with Pippa at one of the restaurant bars here the last time I was in Houston, though."

"Why would you guys drink at a hotel bar?"

"Pippa says it's a good place to meet interesting people from out of town," she says with a shrug, returning her attention to me.

"I guess she's got a point there," I admit. "Although I would argue that *you're* an interesting person from out of town."

"It's hard to have a conversation on the dancefloor," she replies. Then she elbows me and nods to someone approaching us. "Is that our guy?"

Sure enough, Ryan's walking toward us, the lights built

into the awning we're standing under casting harsh shadows over his face; I almost don't recognize him.

"Tom!" Ryan says, starting to look more like himself the closer he gets to us. He's approaching me with his hand out. When I accepted it, he asks, "How was the drive?"

"It was fine," I reply, letting go of him and looking over at Michelle. I reach out, letting my fingertips and the heel of my palm rest on her lower back. "Ryan, this is my wife, Michelle."

"Thank you for inviting us," Michelle says sweetly, indulging in his need to exchange handshakes. "I've been dying to get away from work."

"I'm more than happy to give you the excuse," Ryan says, letting his arm fall to his side. "It's nice to meet you. I was starting to think Tom made you up."

To me, that feels like an accusation, but Michelle just laughs and leans into me, telling Ryan, "Wouldn't be the first time I've heard that. I wonder what it is about Tom that makes people think that."

And like that, the tense moment, if that's even what this was, passes. Ryan reaches into the pocket of his tan blazer and produces a folded slip of paper that he hands to me.

"Itinerary," he says by way of explanation. "We've only got the two things, but we're training an intern and," he trails off, shrugging instead of finishing his sentence. "Your room key's tucked in there, too. I'm pretty sure you're on the twenty-second floor."

"How's the view?" Michelle asks.

"I didn't personally inspect it, but I think it's hard to have a bad view that far up," he says. "If the room isn't to your liking, have your husband let me know, and I'll see what I can do for you."

My brain catches on that word, husband. I know that's the

game we're playing, a show we're putting on for Ryan in an attempt to get him to trust me with his company, but it's jarring hearing myself referred to like that.

On the plus side, I think he buys it.

"I'm not *that* picky," she assures him. "I'm sure it's perfect."

Ryan smiles at her; it's genuine and open. He *likes* her. I don't know if I'm completely sold on this being a good idea, but I'm growing more optimistic every second.

"Still, if it's less than perfect, let us know," he insists as he pulls his phone out of his pants pocket. "I'll let you guys head up there and get comfortable. My wife's calling me. I'll see you two in a few hours. I can't wait for you to meet everyone."

"We're looking forward to it," I say as I step away from Michelle to grab my bag.

Her hand stops me from getting too far, though, her thin fingers catching my wrist, her palm sliding down against mine. I'm careful to keep the surprise out of my face when I turn to look at her.

Michelle's completely at ease, smiling at Ryan until he turns around, raising his phone to his ear as he walks away. She doesn't let go, even after he walks off.

"Here," she says, holding my bag out toward me. I have to shove the room key into my pocket before accepting it. She bends down to get her own from the ground before pulling me toward the lobby, saying, "Let's see what kind of view we have."

I let her lead me into the lobby. She slows down to look at the Texas-shaped chandelier but keeps walking, making a beeline for the front desk. However, she changes her mind when she spots the elevators, hidden by the concierge station and tucked behind a giant cream-colored wall.

I'm not sure why I'm surprised she's so confident – I've seen her at work. She's probably just employing that personality here. Or, my mind supplies in a dangerous whisper, she's not putting this on, and she's being herself. I shake my head, putting an end to that line of thinking. That's how my harmless crush turns into an all-consuming thing.

"What's our room number again?" she asks as she presses the call button.

"Uh," I reply, dropping my bag to fish the room key out of my pocket. "Twenty-two oh five."

She watches me with a sly smile on her face that doesn't go away, even after I'm done adjusting the strap of my duffle on my shoulder. We step onto the elevator, and she drops my hand, and all of a sudden, I realize why she is smiling at me.

I jerk my head away from her, fixing my gaze on a smudge on the mirrored walls. She doesn't say anything until we start going up.

"What time is dinner? I didn't eat before you picked me up."

"You could have said something," I reply, frowning at her. "Stopping wouldn't have been an issue."

She shrugs. "Maybe I didn't want to spoil my dinner."

I snort before I say, "Spoil your dinner?"

"Shut up," she snaps playfully, stepping through the doors before they're fully opened. "I had a late breakfast."

I roll my eyes and follow her down the hallway. "Dinner's at seven."

"That's an entire hour away," she groans, stopping in front of our door.

"We're eating in the building. We could get there early and order an appetizer before everyone else shows up," I say, unlocking the door and holding it open so she can walk in first.

actually together. Isn't the saying that the best lies are based on the truth?

"Wait, really?" Ryan asks, looking excitedly between Tom and me. "That's so romantic."

"I was going to say it's sexy," Andrea says at the same time our server reappears to drop off my drink.

He walks off, an amused look on his face; I can't help but wonder what other conversations he's overheard working here.

"It's a mix of both," I say, taking a sip and finding that this margarita is somehow stronger than the last one. "I'm the sexy one."

"Damn right you are," Tom says, and I have to remind myself that he's only flirting for the sake of the people around us.

"Aw," Andrea coos. "Tom, does that mean you're the romantic one."

"Disgustingly so," I say, pursing my lips and scrunching my nose in false disgust. "A real charmer, too."

"Why are you saying that like it's a bad thing?" Tom asks. "I thought you liked the romantic dates I take you on."

"You're right," I concede. "I do like them, but that's only because I like you, you giant cheeseball."

I might be overdoing it, but everyone at the table is laughing, so I choose not to worry about it. Tom makes a show of reaching over to squeeze my upper thigh under the table. The action's all for show, but it sends very real tendrils of arousal into my stomach. His hand lingers there for what feels like a second too long, but I know better.

I put down my margarita and reach for my water. The alcohol's great for loosening up, but I need to stay in control of my actions. I'm already forgetting that Tom isn't actually my partner. I still have to make it through drinks with Andrea.

"So," Tom says, leaning back and looking truly at ease for the first time tonight, "how did you two meet?"

"Oh, us?" Andrea asks, looking over at Ryan. "High school sweethearts."

"No!" I say, glancing between the two of them.

"Yep," Jason says, apparently unhappy at being left out of the discussion. "They were each other's first everything. If you want to talk about disgusting…" he gestures wildly between Andrea and Ryan.

"Jason's just bitter. Ignore him," Andrea says.

"Oh, screw you," he replies. "I'm not bitter."

"He's right," Ryan says. "He actually just hates love."

"If you hate love, what are you doing working on an app for families?" I ask; I've gathered that Jason takes teasing well. "That doesn't make any sense."

"I'm a sellout," Jason says, shrugging. "Ryan provides a paycheck, so here I am."

"You know what," I say, careful to keep my eyes off of Tom, "I *totally* get what you mean. Whatever pays the bills."

"Amen," he says, raising his beer in my direction.

I toast him with my water, grinning when Andrea raises her drink, too. The amount of "cheersing" these people do is kind of astounding. I'm not complaining, though. There's a real sense of camaraderie here. I bet this is the kind of company that says they're all family and actually means it.

I really hope what I'm doing here helps Tom land a contract with them. These are good people.

Ryan gets the bill as our conversation turns away from personal to something a little more business oriented. I stop understanding most of what they're saying; right now, they're talking about a user interface. It's all over my head.

"You two can run off to the bar," Ryan says, apparently

remembering Andrea and I are still here. "We'll catch up with you."

"I'm waiting for Michelle to finish her drink," Andrea says, pulling her straw from her glass and sticking it in mine.

"By all means," I laugh, "help yourself."

"I'm trying to help you," she says. "Let's finish it together."

I lean in, grabbing my own straw between my pointer finger and thumb, waiting for Andrea to assume her position. She holds her body with a silly kind of confidence; she's walking on the edge of drunk but is still completely there. And while we're gulping the drink down, I'm reminded of Pippa.

Shit. I need to see what Pippa's doing. I bet she'd love Andrea. Maybe she'll meet us here.

"Alright," Andrea says, standing up and pulling her purse onto her shoulder, "I see two seats right over there with our names on them. Come on, Michelle, kiss your husband goodbye."

I blink, my brain moving slowly, and when I finally turn my head to face Tom, he's already looking at me, almost like a deer in headlights. I'm very aware of the eyes on us, so I cup his cheek and draw him forward into a chaste kiss before I can think too hard about it.

"I'll see you later; good luck," I say when I pull away, ignoring the butterflies that flutter in my stomach.

I thank god I'm able to make my escape, even if I have to hover near Andrea while she presses a kiss on Ryan's cheek. My face is hot, and I can't look Tom in the eye. If I were to speak right now, it would come out clipped and tight.

When we get settled onto the barstools, I eagerly order another margarita. Andrea seconds it and slides Ryan's card across the bartop. They come, and we finish them, talking about where we grew up – Andrea and Ryan were both born and raised in Houston.

When the second round of drinks gets to us, I discuss my failed relationships before my "successful" one with Tom. Andrea shyly admits that Ryan is her one and only serious boyfriend and that she's never even kissed anyone else.

"I wonder what that's like," I say out loud, the filter between my brain and mouth not working quite the way I want it to.

She cocks her head to the side and says, "You wonder what what's like?"

I pick my words carefully, realizing I've made a mistake and have almost revealed too much, saying, "Doing it right on the first try."

"Oh, that," she says, smiling down at her drink. "It's just dumb luck, honestly."

"No, Andrea," I say with conviction. "That's like… It's like you guys are *soulmates*."

"You think you and Tom aren't?"

"I didn't say that," I correct her quickly. "You and Ryan meeting so young and only being with each other… that seems divine. It's like the universe planned it or something."

"I like that," she says thoughtfully after a beat. "Divine."

I squirm a little under the weight of her gaze. While I'm pretty sure I said the exact right thing; I'm not sure what to do with her attention. Talking about relationships is something I don't really have a lot of experience in.

"I think all relationships are little acts of the universe," she says, finally looking away from me. "Even all those ones you had that didn't work out."

Even the ones that are all for show?

"Huh."

"You and Tom meeting at your job is like that too," she

says. "Didn't you say you started about a month after he started coming in?"

"I did," I confirm.

"That, my friend, is the universe," she declares.

I'm already instinctively picking up my cup to clink with hers.

"We're friends?"

She looks at me like I'm insane and says, "Duh. You're, like, the most fun person I've ever met."

"You're just saying that," I say.

"No, I mean it," she insists. Then, she lights up and grabs my arm excitedly, "You should come dancing with us after this."

"That's not on the itinerary," I giggle, almost bubbling over with the joy of drunk-girl friendship. "But I think I'll be able to find the time."

"Fuck yes, you can!" she claims, then something catches her eye. "Oh, look. Our boys!"

I turn around, following her line of sight, and sure enough, Tom, Ryan, and Jason are walking toward us, laughing about something. From the looks of it, their meeting went well, and I'm overcome by the urge to go to Tom and wrap my arms around him.

Then I remember we're fake-married. I can if I want, and it won't even be weird. So, I get up, the room tilting a little and my legs shaky. He meets me in the middle, catching me with strong arms. I let myself get lost in this little game we're playing and lean my head on his shoulder.

"How'd it go?" I whisper in his ear, grinning wickedly when he shivers.

"Good," Tom replies, resting his hands on my waist when I pull away. "Did you have fun with Andrea?"

"Oh my gosh," I say, squeezing his biceps. "We're friends now. *And* she invited us to go dancing with her."

"What about Pippa?" he asks, bringing my rushing, drunk mind to an abrupt halt.

"Shit," I say, pulling my phone out of my pocket. There are notifications with Pippa's name on them, but I can't read them. "Here, can you call her and let her know we're going dancing with Andrea."

"Yeah," he says, accepting my phone. "Um, where are we going? So I can tell her where to meet us."

"She has my location," I say, waving him off and stepping away to join Andrea at the bar again. "She'll need time to get ready, anyway. So just let her know we're going dancing."

CHAPTER 6
Tom

Michelle's friend seemed way less than amused when I let her know we were going dancing. She was even less amused when I couldn't tell her the name of the club. I like to think that all of Pippa's frustration was aimed at Michelle, but that would be naïve. She blames me as much, if not more, than she blames Michelle.

Not that it matters now; Michelle's been tearing up the dance floor with Andrea for the better part of an hour, only appearing to gulp down water and take little sips of her drink. I half-wish she would stick around and join in the conversation. I miss her.

Actually, it's like the universe read my mind or something. When I look away from the conversation Ryan and Jason are having, Andrea is pulling Michelle to the table. Her eyes are glued to her husband, and even though I can't hear her, I can tell Michelle is giggling wildly.

I tap Ryan's elbow to get his attention and then point at the girls approaching us. He whips his head up, following my line of sight.

"God, they're beautiful, aren't they?" he asks when he

spots his wife.

"Yeah," I reply without even thinking, my eyes glued to Michelle.

It's been surprisingly easy playing her husband. She's been doing most of the work, initiating touches and tossing affectionate words my way, but I've been getting bolder as the night goes on. I let my hands linger and don't hide how I stare at her body.

The confidence might be all of the alcohol, though.

Ryan and I worked out a deal earlier, something that should be very lucrative for both of us, and we've been *celebrating* ever since. So, I'm not wasted, but one wrong move, and I'll be there. So, I should probably slow down before I embarrass myself.

I take another sip from my glass, putting it back onto its coaster to calm my nerves before the women get back.

"You ladies having fun?" Jason, who's somehow the soberest of us all, asks when they arrive at our table.

"The *most* fun," Andrea says, opting to pluck Ryan's drink from his hand instead of grabbing her own. "This DJ is incredible."

"Do you think he travels?" Michelle asks me, sliding into the booth.

Our bodies touch from shoulder to hip, and she's warm against me. It only feels natural to put my arm around her. We fit together perfectly, and I'm sure the maneuver looks practiced.

"He'd be a hit at Metro," I say, knowing where her line of questioning was heading. "You should get his name when you guys go back out there. Jake's been looking for fresh talent."

"You and Ryan are coming with us," Andrea declares, inserting herself into our conversation, still standing at the head of the table.

"In a minute, though," Michelle promises me, patting my arm and finishing her water. "I need a break."

"Weak," Andrea laughs, shoving at Ryan's shoulder so he'll make room for her. When she's seated in the booth next to him, she asks, "So, what've you guys been talking about? Work?"

"That was two songs ago," Ryan jokes, looking at her tenderly. "We're talking about the pros and cons of being a Cowboys fan."

"Geeze," she says, rolling her eyes before fixing me with a piercing gaze. "Don't tell me you're a Cowboys fan."

"Guilty," I laugh, lifting my free hand in surrender.

"Aren't you from Houston? Why the hell wouldn't you be a Texans fan?" she cries, her eyes widening comically.

"His dad's from Dallas," Michelle interjects, seamlessly coming to my rescue with a piece of information I didn't even know she had. "He's got a sentimental attachment to the Cowboys."

"And you guys are picking on him?" Andrea says, apparently on whatever side Michelle is. "I'm disappointed."

"You're not that disappointed," Ryan replies, pressing a kiss to Andrea's cheek.

She looks at him, unimpressed, for a beat before looking back at me.

"What brought your dad to Houston?"

"My mom, mostly," I reply. "They both went to school at the University of Houston, but her family's from around here."

"Really?" Jason asks. "If you've got all this family here, why are you in Austin?"

"Got stuck there after school," I say, feeling Michelle's eyes on me; she's never heard this story before. All the guys I work with have already heard it a thousand times. "Well, not really stuck. I got a job in the city and never made it around to moving back here."

"So it was in the plan?" Ryan asks.

"At one point, yeah," I say before glancing at Michelle. "I have a reason to stay there now, though."

"That's so sweet," Michelle says, her voice sounding a little funny. "But I don't have a problem with Houston."

"Yeah?" I ask, "You think a Houston move is in our future?"

She hums, barely audible over the thrum of the music, and taps her fingers against my thigh thoughtfully. She considers the question like it's a real possibility, us moving out here together. I wonder if she's still putting on a show or if she's actually considering it.

"Pippa's here," she says. "And maybe, if we moved here, she'd *actually* meet us out."

"I told you earlier that she wasn't feeling up to it," I remind her.

I'm fully aware that I shouldn't have lied to Michelle, but in my defense, she was already drunk when we left the hotel to get here. She'll get the truth tomorrow morning when we're both sober. Until then, Pippa is sick, and we're having fun despite that.

"I *know* that," Michelle says, but she clearly doesn't believe it. She probably knows more about why Pippa stayed home than I do. "It'd be convenient, though."

"You heard the woman," Jason says, knocking against my shoulder. "It's time to start looking for a new place."

"Ugh, can we stop talking and get back on the dance-floor?" Andrea cuts in impatiently. "The music's too loud for talking."

"Please," Michelle groans, sliding out of the booth. She offers me her hand and says, "Come on, baby, let's dance."

I take her hand, my head feeling fuzzy with booze and the use of the pet name. She yanks me to my feet, and then we're off, weaving through a crowd of tightly packed, sweaty bodies.

I rarely leave my table at Metro, so being on the dance floor is new to me. The music's so much louder here, sending vibrations directly into my core in a not-unpleasant way. And, as Michelle hauls us closer to the speakers, I feel like I've stepped into the music like I'm an integral part of the composition.

"I love this song," she says, her voice barely audible above the noise. "I hate that I can't dance to it at work."

"Who said you can't dance?" I ask, placing my free hand on her waist.

"No one," she replies, dropping my wrist and putting her arms around my neck. "I'm just sure it'd affect my tips."

"Nonsense," I reply, imagining her being this free on the clock. "I think you'd get better tips.

"I'm a bottle girl, not a stripper," she says, bouncing along in time with the beat. "I have no idea how to dance if we're being completely honest here."

"You look fine," I say. "I'd tip you more if I saw you having this much fun at work."

"That's because you're my husband," she drawls, leaning in close. "I'd expect the best tips from you."

"Well, you know me. I have to take care of my wife financially," I reply, indulging in this fantasy.

I know no one else can hear us, but I cannot help but play along. What can I say? It's fun having a wife.

"Mm, sweetheart," she says, putting her mouth right next to my ear, "taking care of me financially would be paying all my bills. If you were really taking care of me, I'd be able to quit my job."

And I don't know what it is, her proximity, the alcohol, or the fact that we've been playing husband and wife all night, but I can't stop myself from saying, "I can make that happen. Say the word, and I can make it happen."

Michelle pulls away from me then her head cocked to the side. I think she might laugh and put an end to this little game we're playing, but after a moment, she smiles wide and brightly.

"Does that mean I don't have to work when we move here?" she asks, leaning back into me.

I laugh and say, "You don't have to work when we get back if you don't want to."

"Now, don't say that," she replies. "I might actually take you up on that offer."

"Fine by me," I say, and it's mostly the truth. "You want me to talk to Jake for you?"

"Nah," she says happily, a mischievous twinkle in her eye.

Then, the DJ transitions into a Doja Cat song, and Michelle all but yells in excitement. She steps away from me, claiming more room for herself, and I let my arms fall to my sides, watching in amusement as she sways her hips and runs her fingers through her hair.

I don't know the words, but she does, her mouth moving fast and hitting every syllable. I'm enjoying the show, and then she turns around. I think she's about to walk away and create more distance between us initially, but she surprises me by backing up.

It takes a second to realize what she's doing, but when I do, I grab onto her hips and pull her ass against me. The smell of her perfume fills my nose, and she covers my hands with hers and starts moving.

I try to match her rhythm, but I can't. There's a skill in her movements that only comes from dancing like this often. I wonder how often she goes out with her friends, how often she dances like this with other guys. I wonder if they're better at this than I am.

That thought has to be stamped out, jealousy rising in my throat like bile. It doesn't *matter* if Michelle gets this close to other people. I don't have a real claim on her; our "marriage" is just for show. None of this is real.

Her body against mine, though, that's real, and I let myself enjoy it as much as I dare — I don't think Michelle will love it if I get hard on the dance floor. It's difficult to do with the way she's moving.

I keep myself under control for the next few songs, enjoying her closeness, but not too much. I almost lose track of time out here, and I find myself imagining what it might be like if this was something we did all the time.

The way she's dancing and clearly enjoying herself, I'm sure this would be a common occurrence. This isn't usually my thing, but I'm enjoying myself way more than expected. I'm almost positive we would stay until the lights come on on the dance floor more often than not.

If I weren't so tired from the drive, I'm pretty sure we would be here until closing the club closed tonight. I'm tempted to stay here all night anyway, but I will have to stop the fun soon, even though I don't want to. I still have to drive us back to Austin tomorrow morning.

God, my hangover's going to be hell. It's probably best that I'm not sleep-deprived, too.

"Michelle," I mutter against her ear; I'm close enough that only she can hear. "I think it's about time for us to get outta here."

She turns around slowly; her eyes focused on my mouth. I think about kissing her, but I don't, waiting for her to make a move. In my mind, I'm screaming at her to kiss me, but after a long beat, she looks away from my lips.

"We need to say goodbye to our friends," she says, and I'm unable to identify the tone in her voice again.

"They're probably back at the table," I reply, my view of our seats obscured by the thick crowd. "Wanna get back there?"

"Sure," she says, offering me her hand.

I take it, lacing our fingers together and weaving back to our table where Ryan, Andrea, and Jason sit, sipping on mostly full drinks. When we come to a stop in front of them, Michelle leans against me, her head on my shoulder.

"You two doing shots?" Jason asks, face brightening at the sight of us.

"I don't think so," I say, regretting the fact that I have to say no. "We're actually about to head out."

"So soon?" Andrea whines. "It's not even midnight."

"I know, I know," I console her. "We gotta get out of here early tomorrow. Michelle works tomorrow night."

"God, don't remind me," she groans, nuzzling into my neck.

I have to pretend the action doesn't make my heart beat wildly against my ribs. There's no way I can deny the urge to wrap my arm around her and squeeze her closer.

"Sorry to see you go so soon," Ryan says. "I'll be in touch Monday."

"I'll keep an eye on my email," I promise.

"We'll see you soon," Andrea says. "Be safe."

"We will," Michelle promises, lifting her head. "Come on, Tom. You wanna order an Uber?"

CHAPTER 7
Michelle

I think I've given up on trying to get Tom to make a move on me. I've been as forward as I can be the entire night, and still, he's been respectable and treated this as the business transaction it is. We're sitting on opposite sides of the Uber, a clear indication that our charade is over.

We're just friends again. And that's fine.

Now that I'm starting to sober up, I'm a little embarrassed by the way I acted. I'd be even more embarrassed, but Tom seemed to be enjoying the time we spent together while we were there. Maybe that was the alcohol, though. I guess I can't be too sure.

I look at him now; his face is illuminated by the buildings as we fly by them. He's handsome, his face clean-shaven, his jawline boyish. It occurs to me that he looks much younger than he is, that we could probably pass for the same age if we really wanted to.

"Is there something on my face?" he asks, noticing my eyes on him.

"No," I say, shaking my head as my face starts to get

warm. I don't have an excuse for staring, so I don't offer one. "I'm just thinking about the shower back in the room."

"The water pressure is incredible," he says, grinning at me. "I'm looking forward to my shower before we leave tomorrow."

I roll my eyes, smirking at him, "You're so lame. You know that, right?"

"I'm the lame one?" he asks. "You're the one sitting here, zoning out, thinking about the shower."

"Whatever," I laugh. He has a point. "How'd the meeting go? I know you guys closed on a deal or whatever."

"We did," he says. "And it went well. Ryan's super passionate about FamFirst. I think he's going to be a dream to work with. He and Andrea have a six-month-old daughter."

"I think I remember Andrea telling me that," I say; I vaguely remember her mentioning a child, but not her age or name.

"They struggled with infertility for a long time," he continues. "Beth, their daughter, she's an IVF baby. Ryan started developing the app as soon as they found out Andrea was pregnant."

"That's sweet," I say, wishing I'd have given Andrea the space to tell me about her baby.

"Isn't it?" Tom says, looking back out the window at the groups of people leaving the bars.

"So, where do your guys come in?" I ask.

Tom's job involves a lot of technical terms that I don't understand; it might be nice having an idea of what he does.

"We come in and improve the user interface," he says. "There's also some back-end stuff I think we can improve, too. Ryan's got a good product; we're just going to streamline it."

"Very cool," I say. Then, because I don't like the silence

that falls over us, I add, "So, bringing me along was worth it?"

"So worth it," he laughs. I find myself wanting to hear him laugh more. "Although they adored you, so I might have to bring you along if we ever have another in-person meeting."

"Will I be compensated for my time?" I ask, mostly joking.

Truthfully, I think I'd do this for free. I didn't pay for anything all night and had a blast going out with everyone.

"Of course," Tom says like it shouldn't even be a question. "I'm not trying to mess with your cash flow. If you're missing work to help me out, you'll get paid."

"Well, if you want to put me on payroll, I wouldn't say no."

"I'll talk to accounting when we get back," he promises, and I actually believe him.

We lapse into another silence, but this time it's comfortable. I wish I wasable to reach out and grab his hand, my brain still stuck in the moment from earlier. Although, I don't think he'd mind if I did that.

By tomorrow morning, everything between us will be back to normal, though. So, there's no point in doing something right now that might make tomorrow awkward.

It only takes a few more minutes for us to get to the hotel, our driver pulling up to the door and wishing us a good evening as we climb out of the car.

Tom walks ahead of me, holding the front door open. I walk through, and he falls into step beside me. I think he's going to put his hand on my back, but he doesn't, and I have to act like I'm not disappointed.

I lead him to the elevators wordlessly, my heels clicking on the cream concrete floor. The lights are so bright compared to the darkness outside that everything looks white and out of focus. I squint at the employee sitting at the front desk and give her a half-smile when she nods in greeting.

"You have the key, right?" I ask when I press the elevator call button, nudging Tom with my elbow.

"Uh," he mutters, pulling his wallet from his pocket. He opens it a little frantically, but his shoulders relax immediately as he pulls it out and says, "Right here."

"I figured you had it," I laugh as the doors open. "Sorry if I freaked you out."

Tom doesn't say anything; he just slips his wallet back into his pocket, keeping the room key in his hand like he's afraid it'll disappear.

"Hey," I say, stepping onto the elevator before the doors are fully open, my head inclined toward him, "I wasn't *that* worried. There's someone at the desk."

"Yeah, but I don't know if my name's on the reservation," he explains. "We might have had to call Ryan, and who knows if he would have been able to hear us."

I find myself laughing even though it's not funny; we're just talking about nothing. There's something strangely domestic about this moment. If I were an onlooker, I'd think this was something he and I do all the time. I'd see the rings on our fingers and assume we're happily married.

It's a nice thought, actually.

Tom leads me down the hallway to our room, unlocking the door and then holding it open for me to step through. The door closes behind us, and I realize I've been so focused on getting into the shower that I forgot I'm sharing the bed with him tonight.

He doesn't seem too bothered by it, kicking off his shoes and loosening his tie. Then he says, "Mind if I get in there before you shower?"

"That's fine," I say, determined to remain as neutral about this as possible.

Tom's quick in the bathroom, only in there long enough to change and brush his teeth. He flops onto the bed without a glance in my direction, reading something on his phone. I carefully don't look at him as I gather my pajamas from where they're folded on the bed and dart into the bathroom.

I take my time, partly because the water pressure *is* amazing, but mostly because I'm inexplicably nervous about sharing the bed with him. Of course, we've kept our hands to ourselves since we left the bar, but still…

It's ridiculous, honestly.

There's not even a chance of anything happening. We're *just* going to sleep. And then, when we wake up tomorrow, we're (hopefully) going to get breakfast and drive home. Tom will go back to being my regular. I'll go back to barely making ends meet. Everything's going to be normal again.

But, my mind says, *how are things going to be normal again when you know how his lips taste?*

I shove my head under the stream of water to drown out the noise.

Eventually, I admit to myself I've been in here long enough and cut the shower off. Then, I dry myself off, and I slip into soft shorts and a tank top. Before I leave the bathroom, I scrunch my hair in the towel, squeezing out the excess water; I don't like going to sleep with wet hair.

Snoring comes from the direction of the bed, and I realize Tom's out cold. As it turns out, I was worrying for nothing. There's no awkward conversation and no lying next to him, knowing we're both awake and waiting for the other person to fall asleep.

I repack my duffel bag, pulling out my clothes for tomorrow and tossing them on the couch. Then, I grab the plastic cups next to the coffee maker and fill them with water from the bathroom sink. Finally, I throw the comforter back and crawl in, keeping myself on the edge of the bed despite its size.

The sheets rustle beneath me as I settle in after I click the light off. When I finally find a comfortable position more than an arm's length away from Tom, the only sound left in the room is his deep, even breathing.

I stare up at the ceiling, the lights of the city casting a blue hue over everything. All at once, I feel very alone, like I'm the only person on this planet. My breath is knocked out of me as I grapple with the intensity of the feeling.

It's not true. Obviously, I'm not the only person here. Tom's sleeping next to me. But the loneliness is deeper than that; it's in my bone marrow, intrinsically part of me. I am profoundly alone.

I have Pippa, but I'm doing everything in my power to mess that up. She didn't come out tonight, and that's my fault. Tom said she was sick, but I know she's probably pissed at me, and rightfully so. For whatever reason, I got drunk and ditched her for my new friends.

I'll have to kiss her ass and make up for this for the next week, I'm sure.

She can't fill the void I'm carrying in me, though. For one, she lives two hours away, and we both work so often that we only see each other once a month. If that. And two, I crave a kind of intimacy I know she can't give me.

I want someone to care about me. I want a boyfriend. I want romance.

It's the alcohol and this stupid act Tom, and I put on. I know that. I only ever feel like this when I'm drinking. Historically, boyfriends have been nothing more than an expense and a headache. I'm better off alone, and that's something I wholeheartedly believe.

But after tonight, maybe I'm not so sure.

Almost every relationship I've been in has been short-lived and fraught with anxiety. It's not like I had any positive examples of relationships growing up, either. My parents got divorced when I was eight, and Mom's been in and out of relationships ever since. So this is the first time I've ever seen a couple in a long-term relationship look happy in real life.

This is the first time I've ever let myself seriously think about consciously loving and being loved. The idea is nice in theory, but I'm not sure how well it would work in practice. Trusting another person with that much of myself is terrifying. I don't think I'm wired for something like that; too independent for my own good.

Most of what I felt when I was with Tom could probably be attributed to the fact that we were playing pretend. The stakes weren't very high, at least not emotionally, but it felt so natural. It was almost like he and I were supposed to be together or something.

I sigh, rolling to face Tom fully. All I can see in the dark is the silhouette of his profile. Still, he's handsome, his nose strong and his cheeks soft. His lips, which I kissed earlier in the evening, look just as pillowy and inviting in the low light.

If I were allowed, I'd reach out and touch him. I'd lie my head on his chest and let his heartbeat lull me to sleep. I might even tangle my fingers in the soft fabric of his shirt as I drift out of consciousness.

I'm not allowed, though. So, after I get my fill and memorize the lines of his face, I roll away. Sleep comes slowly, but before the world finally fades away, I think I feel Tom shifting closer to me.

CHAPTER 8
Tom

Before I even open my eyes, I can tell something's off. Not wrong, but off. I'm way warmer than usual, and there's a solid weight on my chest. Troublingly, there's hair in my mouth, and even more troubling, I can't see anything when I finally crack an eyelid.

I'm about to push the weight away when I remember the night before and where I am.

Michelle and I shared the bed. And, at some point, while we were sleeping, she rolled on top of me. I know she rolled on top of me because I'm still in the same place I was when I fell asleep.

Carefully, I reach up and push her hair out of my face. I squint against the bright light streaming in from the window and look down at the top of her head. Her long lashes are fanned against her cheeks, and her mouth is open so very slightly as she snores softly. Her body rises and falls in time with my breathing.

She stirs in my arms but doesn't wake up. In fact, she sighs deeply, and the hand she has tangled in my shirt loosens as she gets more comfortable. She slides one of her legs between mine, putting even more of her body weight on me.

My brain is running on overdrive; I have a couple of different options here. First, and probably most advisable, is waking Michelle up. It wouldn't have to be a big deal or weird. But that would involve saying something that isn't totally weird.

My second option is to somehow separate the two of us without waking her up. That feels like an impossible feat. She and I are wrapped in each other, our legs tangled. I'm not even sure how to begin the task. Maybe if I try to roll over–

"Tom?"

Shit. That's the third option. Wait until she wakes up on her own. It's the one I was hoping to avoid.

"Morning," I say, trying my best to sound unbothered by our current position. Then, because apparently, I want to act like this isn't happening, I say, "How did you sleep?"

Michelle is quiet for what feels like too long, but she stays where she is when she answers, "Better than I have in a long time."

"Yeah?" I ask, not quite sure what's going on here.

She nods, her cheek rubbing against my chest, the hairs on the top of her head tickling my nose. My innocent little crush threatens to burn into something dangerous. This entire situation feels like we're walking on a tightrope.

"How did you sleep?" she murmurs after a moment, rubbing a circle with her thumb mindlessly against my pec. I'm sure she can hear my heart pounding out of my chest below her ear.

I consider her question while I try to get myself under control. Now that I've recovered from the initial shock of waking up with someone else, I'm feeling good; great, even. I've got a little bit of a hangover, but other than that, I think that might have been one of the best nights of sleep I've ever gotten in my life.

"I slept alright," I say nonchalantly, downplaying how well I actually slept.

She hums, content to stay where she is. I wonder who's going to break the spell, how long this can realistically last. Selfishly, I hope we stay like this for longer. But, even more selfishly, I want more. I want to kiss her. I want to rake my fingers through her hair. I want to feel every part of her.

This does have to end, though, and that reality comes crashing down on me when she lifts her head to look me in the eyes. I gaze up at her, feeling exposed like I'm being looked right through, and I think I might be blushing like a teenager. She's in my space, sharing my breath, just *staring*.

I think I know what's about to happen, what she's about to do. I've been with enough women to know where this is going. My throat clicks when I swallow, my mouth dry, my tongue too big for my mouth. Her eyes dart down to my lips and then back up.

"Can I?" Michelle asks.

I can't seem to form a coherent sentence, so I nod and lean forward, smiling into the kiss when she meets me in the middle. Her lips are plush and warm, inviting me in and asking me to stay awhile.

It's different from the kiss we shared last night. There's an intensity here that wasn't there before, an understanding between the two of us. Whatever this is, it's not a performance or some game. It's real.

She licks into my mouth as she adjusts herself on top of me, straddling my lap. There's no hiding the fact that I'm already a little hard, a mixture of my not completely shrunk morning wood and her persistent mouth. Maybe I should be embarrassed, but this is like something out of a wet dream; I can't find it in myself to be too ashamed of how into this, how into *her*, I am.

I satiate my desire to get my hands into her luscious, brown hair. It's just as soft as I imagined it would be, when I gently stroke my thumb along her scalp, she all but purrs into my mouth. If I were braver, I'd tangle my fingers here and pull, but I'm not sure what this means or how we got here. I'm afraid of doing something that would put a stop to where this is going.

Michelle deepens the kiss, angling her head and sticking her tongue into my mouth. I suck at her tongue experimentally, and she pulls away, her face flushed and her lips wet. She watches me carefully; then, excruciatingly slowly, she grinds her hips into my hard cock, and her eyes fall closed as she does so.

"I think we should have sex."

The words are out of my mouth before I even realize what I'm saying. Above me, Michelle giggles, letting her forehead come down to rest on top of mine.

"Yeah," she whispers, the words making my already hot body even warmer, "that's what I was trying to do."

Something between a laugh and a huff escapes my mouth, and then she kisses me again. This time she's more confident, cupping my jaw and pulling me against her. I'm more than willing to be guided by her. We melt into each other with lazy, tender movements.

I know this is our first time doing this, but it doesn't feel like it. Everything about her body is new, but I know her soul. And when her hands start to roam down my body, I'm sure she feels the same way.

Her fingers ghost over my biceps and then move onto my chest with excited enthusiasm. They continue their journey lower as she continues to kiss me thoroughly. She stops at the top of my sweatpants, pulling away from my mouth and hooking her pointer fingers in the waistband.

I let her undress me, lifting myself off the bed slightly as she pulls off my pants and boxers in one motion. She eyes my cock hungrily as it slaps against my stomach, tossing my clothes aside and reaching for her own shorts.

With grace, she slips out of them, and then we're both naked from the waist down. Her lips are back on mine before I can get a good look at her. I already regret not seeing her.

This time, she's holding herself up with one hand and has another between our bodies, resting on my shirt as she kisses me senseless. My head swims, and every single one of my senses are overtaken by her. I'm so focused on her tongue against my teeth that I'm not expecting it when her hand wraps around my dick.

"Shit," I hiss into Michelle's mouth as she jerks me off, scrambling to grab onto her.

"That feel good?" she asks, her voice low and sultry as she continues to pump her hand up and down.

I can't do anything but nod, which seems to be an adequate response because she speeds her movements up a little. My hips jerk forward involuntarily, chasing the contact and desperate for more.

"I'm going to ride you now," she says, pulling away from my mouth with a loud pop.

"Wait," I say as she starts to line my cock up with her cunt. "We need a condom."

"Are you clean?" Michelle asks, holding her position and watching me with a raised eyebrow.

"Well, yeah," I say, earning a peck on the cheek from her.

"So am I," she replies, "and I'm on birth control."

"Okay," I mutter, not quite believing what she's saying.

"So I can ride you?" she asks impatiently.

I barely get a yes out of my mouth before she's sinking onto me agonizingly slowly. When she bottoms out, she takes a second to adjust, breathing hot against my cheek as her body shakes above me.

It takes all of my self-control to keep from thrusting into her; she's warm, tight, and perfect. Eventually, though, she gives me some relief, lifting herself up and sinking back down. My head falls back against the pillow, the sensation steamrolling me.

"You feel incredible," I groan, running my hands up her arms, squeezing just above her elbow.

"You're just saying that," she jokes, gasping as she slams herself down hard. "*Fuck*. You're so big."

Impossibly, I laugh at her joke before I say, "No, you're just saying that."

"Trust me," she says breathlessly, working herself over on my dick, "I wouldn't lie about this for your sake. Your cock is massive."

Those words go right to my head, and I twitch inside her as my orgasm approaches steadily, building just behind my pubic bone. I try to get myself under control, wanting this to last longer and unwilling to come before she does.

She's making beautiful noises, her voice climbing in pitch as she fucks me earnestly, doing all the work and taking care of me. Her attentiveness is so hot. It's like she's determined to get me off before she gets off.

As much as I'm enjoying this, that's not the kind of lover I am, so I kiss her deeply and shift slightly below her. She repositions herself, holding herself above me with her elbows on either side of my head.

I reach one hand down between our bodies to where she's bouncing on my cock, caressing the smooth skin on the inside of her thigh. My hand climbs higher, past where I'm inside her to her clit. I start rubbing firm, tight circles against her, the knuckle of my thumb brushing against my dick as I do.

"Oh," she moans, pulling her mouth away from mine and panting in my ear as she continues grinding down on me. "Oh, keep going. That's it."

Her proximity sends a sharp bolt of pleasure through my body. My hips are moving of their own accord, meeting each one of Michelle's thrusts and filling the room with the sound of skin slapping against skin.

"I'm not going to last much longer," I say, not caring that this is going to be over so quickly.

"Me either," she whines, her hips speeding up as she rubs against my hand. "Keep doing that."

It takes a few more thrusts, and then Michelle's rhythm falters, and she tightens around me. Her fingernails dig into my shoulders so hard I think he might leave marks through my shirt. I keep my hand moving, drawing out her climax, and pump my hips up until my own orgasm washes over me, and I come inside her.

A few seconds later, she collapses on my chest, my cock still inside her. I wiggle my hand free from between us and let it come to rest on her back. My free hand finds purchase in her hair, and then we lie there; the only sounds in the room are our breathing and the air conditioner. I wish we could stay like this all day.

"You need to shower," she says, finally breaking the silence and sounding a lot like she hates that she's doing it.

"I do," I agree, making no move to push her off of me.

Michelle lifts her head to meet my gaze before saying, "How much longer until check out?"

"Uh," I mutter, turning my head so I can see the alarm clock. "Two hours."

"Let me use the bathroom real quick," she says, climbing off of my lap.

She bends over, giving me a show of her ass and impossibly long legs, to pick up her shorts from the floor before she disappears into the bathroom, leaving me alone to wonder if that really happened or if I'm dreaming. I look down at my spent body, then pinch my arm to make sure I'm awake.

I don't get out of bed until I hear the toilet flush, at which point I jump up and scramble to find where my sweats landed. I manage to locate them, and I finish putting them on at the same time that the bathroom door opens.

"It sucks that we don't have time to hit the pool," Michelle says, walking over to the window and looking out over the city.

"Doesn't your apartment community have a pool?" I ask, grabbing my duffle bag from the couch in the corner of the room.

"Yeah, but it doesn't have a Texas-shaped lazy river," she replies, turning toward me with a twinkle in her eye. "Can we at least go up and see it?"

"Sure," I chuckle. Then, before I duck into the bathroom and because I'm still riding the high of having sex with her, I say, "Maybe we can come back and check it out sometime."

CHAPTER 9
Michelle

It's been a little over a month since Tom and I played husband and wife for an evening, and since then, it really feels like things in my life have been going up. My regulars are tipping me better than usual; Pippa accepted my apology for not meeting up with her, I'm finally on top of my bills, and things are great between Tom and me.

We haven't talked about our hookup yet. Both of us have talked around it when he's come to sit in my section, but we haven't had a candid conversation about it. It's not awkward, though. In fact, he's quickly become one of my best friends. We don't see each other outside of Metro, but we text almost every day.

It's mostly Tom sending me videos he finds online, but I've also kept myself up to date on his contract with FamFirst. He and Ryan work well together, even remotely. They haven't launched the redesign of the app yet, but that should be coming up soon, and with it, another opportunity for me to appear as Tom's wife.

As much as I hate to admit it, I'm actually *really* looking forward to playing pretend with him again, and it's not just because of the money. I'm pretty sure I'm starting to develop real feelings for him. He's sweet and funny and has an amazing sense of humor. It feels like I've known him for so much longer than I have; he gets me, and I'm pretty sure I get him.

Still, though, I am looking forward to another paycheck from Tom. I don't feel like I'm drowning anymore, but things can change in an instant. I've known that my entire life. Having money put back in case of an emergency would be a huge weight off my shoulders.

"Michelle?" a high-pitched voice asks, interrupting my quiet time. "Everything okay in here? Horatio said you ran off looking green."

"I'm fine," I reply from inside the bathroom stall. One of the line cooks must have sent Tish to check on me. "I've been feeling a little nauseous. Pretty sure it's PMS."

"That sucks," she says, stepping into the bathroom completely, the door swinging shut behind her. "Do you need to go home?"

"It's not that serious," I promise her, rising from where I'm kneeling. "This happens every month."

"You should talk to your doctor about that," Tish says conversationally. She must not have any tables right now; it's almost two, and the diner's always dead around this time of the afternoon. "Might be PMDD."

"It might be what?" I ask, unsure of why *this* is the conversation she wants to have, as I finally leave the stall.

"Premenstrual dysphoric disorder," she says, leaning against the counter. "My roommate in college had it. Her hormones threw her all out of whack."

"Huh," I reply, not really interested in taking this subject any further.

She keeps talking while I wash my hands, and then she

follows me back to the server station, where I left my apron. I'm not able to get her to leave me alone until a two-top goes down in my section. Even then, I had to ask her to slow down so I could greet them.

Tish and I have been working together at Peggy's Diner for almost three years. She's one of the most conversational people I know. Hell, I'd go as far as to say she's the human embodiment of southern hospitality. Silence is her enemy, and she's always victorious against it.

Normally, I'm unbothered by her antics; I think they make the days go by a little faster. She means well, and she's a consistently positive presence, but PMS has been kicking my ass this month. I've been extra moody and achy. Plus, my stomach's been in knots. Sometimes a bad smell is enough to set me off.

I just hope my period starts soon so I can go back to feeling normal. I've been feeling like a completely different person lately. I say as much later that night when I'm on FaceTime with Pippa.

"Hold on," Pippa says, tearing her eyes away from her computer; she's still at work, finishing a report that one of her property managers forgot to do. "When did you say your period was supposed to start?"

"A week and a half ago," I say, not sure why she sounds so stressed. "You know that doesn't mean anything. I've never been regular."

"I thought birth control was helping with that," she says, furrowing her brow in thought. "Isn't that, like, the whole reason you're on the pill and don't have an IUD?"

"Well, yeah," I reply, still confused about what she's getting at. "I don't think it's a big deal or anything."

"Michelle," Pippa says, sounding annoyed and long-suffering. "You should take a pregnancy test."

"I'm not pregnant," I say immediately, hating the icy feeling that settles in my stomach. "There's no way."

"Oh, so he *didn't* come inside you," she says sarcastically, her tone biting into me. "Sorry, I must have totally made up the part where he raw dogged you. My bad."

"Come on, Pippa," I say, mostly to assure myself and get rid of the horrible anxiety clawing at my sides, "I'm on birth control. I haven't missed a pill. I'm not pregnant."

"I didn't say you were," she replies, looking back at her computer screen. "I'm just saying it wouldn't hurt to take a pregnancy test considering the circumstances."

"I guess you're right," I admit. But, then, because I *really* don't want to think about the possibility of being pregnant anymore, I ask, "How's that report coming?"

"It's fine," she says, happy to move on now that I've admitted she's right. "I'm just making it look pretty."

"There's a reason they pay you the big bucks," I say.

"You're damn right. Shit," she says, her attention snapping back to her phone. "I've got to take this; it's a work call."

"You're good. Love you."

"Love you, t–" she replies, her voice cutting off as she takes the other call.

I roll my eyes, dropping my phone on the kitchen island. Pippa's words haunt me, but there could be any number of reasons my period's late. It could be the fact that I'm still working close to sixty hours a week or that I haven't been eating healthily. Hell, I missed a few days of my pill last week. So maybe that's what's throwing me off.

Before I can get too far along that line of thinking, a text comes in from Tom. I pick it up, welcoming the distraction. I'm hoping for a funny video, but he's asking if I have a minute to talk, so instead of replying, I go ahead and call him.

"Oh, hey, Michelle," Tom says, answering on the second ring. "Didn't think you'd be ready to talk so soon."

"I can call you back," I offer goodnaturedly. "I'm off the rest of the night."

"No, no, now is good!" he says quickly. "I just got out of a meeting with Ryan."

"How'd that go?" I ask, hoping to hear some kind of good news.

"It went well! Really well, actually," he says. "Ryan invited us to another dinner in Houston to meet one of his investors."

"That's awesome. When?" I ask, not bothering to hide my excitement. I don't care if Tom knows I want to hang out with him.

"Next weekend," Tom replies. "They're going to put us up in another hotel. I'll pay you another $2,000. It'll be a good time."

"Sounds like it," I reply, a rush going to my head at the idea of getting that much money again. "I'll have to check with Jake, but that's not going to be a problem."

"Good," he says. "I'm not sure where we're staying yet, but we can make time to go to the pool if you want."

"Unless there's a Texas-shaped lazy river, I don't want it," I tell him very seriously.

"I can see if they're willing to put us up in the Marquis," he offers.

"I'm just joking," I promise, lightening my tone. "Any pool will do."

"That's more like it," he says, and I can tell he's grinning into his phone. Then, after a beat, he asks, "How was your day?"

"It was alright," I say. "I worked at Peggy's this morning, and I was catching up on housework."

"I'm sorry for interrupting you," he says, sounding like he isn't sorry at all.

"Don't worry about it," I say. "I got off the phone with Pippa right before I called you."

"Ah," he says knowledgeably, "so you're putting off doing chores."

"Something like that," I joke, kicking my feet up to settle in. "How was your day?"

"Boring," he says. "Which is a good thing, I guess. It means we didn't run into any major problems."

"Are y'all just focused on FamFirst right now?"

"Mostly, yeah. There's some routine maintenance for some of our other clients, too, but our plates are pretty full with them," he says. I hear a car door shut on the other end, and Tom continues. "Ryan's super ambitious with the launch."

"And you guys aren't?"

"No," he says. "These guys give a fuck about their jobs. They're ambitious with *every* project. It's just refreshing to have a client that's so attentive. It's a lot easier to make design decisions when we know what Ryan likes."

"Sounds ideal," I say, knowing that some of Tom's clients go radio silent during projects; the other day, he told me it's not uncommon for those clients to have the most complaints about the final product.

"It really is," Tom says. "I'm gonna hop off of here and let Ryan know we'll both be there. When I find out where we're staying, I'll let you know."

"Sounds good," I reply, doing a damn good job of hiding my disappointment at our conversation being cut short. "I should probably let Jake know I'll be missing work."

"Let him know I'll stop stealing you away from work soon," Tom says.

"I will," I promise, even though I'm more than happy to ditch Metro to hang out with him. It's more fun, and I get paid more. "I'll talk to you soon."

"Bye, Michelle," Tom says. "Have a good night."

"You, too," I tell him, truly meaning the words.

I'm the one that hangs up, dropping my phone onto my chest when our text conversation fills the screen. There's a giddy smile on my face, and I can't even remember why I was feeling so worried earlier. It was probably just general anxiety about money.

It really feels like that's about to change, though. With the extra cash from this excursion, I should be able to pay off most of my credit cards. I won't be ahead, but I'll be caught up for the first time in almost a year. I can't even fathom what that's going to feel like.

Once I'm on top of everything, I can start thinking about putting money back and finding a more affordable apartment. My lease isn't up anytime soon, but I know I won't need two bedrooms when it is up. If I do the work early, I might not have to move away from downtown.

After a few minutes of daydreaming about having money and not spending an obnoxious amount on my bills, I text Jake to let him know I'll be missing work to help Ryan, and then I get back to cleaning. I don't get very far, though, because when I open my fridge, I'm hit with the smell of something rotting and immediately start gagging.

CHAPTER 10
Tom

"I can't believe they wouldn't let us stay at the Marriott again," Michelle says, adjusting the strap of her dress as we walk into the fancy Italian restaurant for our dinner reservation.

Inside, the walls are painted a cream color that glows warmly under the elaborate glass light fixtures. Most of the tables are small, set up for parties of two. If I didn't know any better, I'd think we were here for a date rather than a business meeting.

"I know you're upset about the lazy river," I say, ignoring the way my stomach flips as she loops her arm around mine, "but I think our room is way better this time. You can't beat that jacuzzi tub."

She sighs and shakes her head, preparing herself to indulge in the same argument we've been having, "Jacuzzi tubs are so unsanitary, Tom. You can't seriously believe they clean them well."

"Come on," I urge playfully, raising my free hand to wave at Ryan, who's standing at a table across the restaurant. "You know you want to get in there tonight."

"Absolutely not," she replies, nodding at the host as we walk past. "*You* can get in the jacuzzi tub tonight, but I'm not letting you into bed unless you shower afterward."

"Okay," I say, my mouth very dry. I'm suddenly at a loss for words.

We're sharing a bed again. I've been *very* aware of that detail since Ryan invited us for another night in Houston. I may have even jerked off to the thought of what might happen while we're here.

Thankfully, we get to our party, and a chorus of greetings keeps my imagination from running too wild and creating a… situation below my belt.

"Michelle!" Andrea cries, rising from her place at the round table next to Ryan and throwing her arms around Michelle.

"Hey, Andrea," Michelle replies, pulling away from me and returning Andrea's embrace. "It's good to see you."

"It's good to see *you*," Andrea says, letting go of her and seriously looking her in the eyes. "We need to exchange numbers."

Michelle doesn't give Andrea a verbal response. Instead, she gestures to their seats and then shoves her hand into her bag in search of her cell phone. I look away from the women to find Ryan watching me with an amused smile on his face.

"Tom," he says kindly, nodding at the open seat beside Michelle and a woman I don't recognize. On the other side of her is an unfamiliar man. Ryan waits until I sit before he continues speaking. "How was the drive?"

"Not too bad. We left earlier this time and managed to miss rush hour."

"How long did it take?" Andrea asks, leaning forward to look at me around Michelle.

"Uh, a little under two hours once we got on the highway," I say, glancing at the man and woman I don't recognize. "Why?"

"I just remembered how insistent Jason was about flying from here to Austin," she says. "And that's just further proof that he's wrong. Flying there is stupid."

"I love Jason," the woman next to me says, "but my *least* favorite thing about him is his insistence on flying everywhere." Then, she looks at Michelle and says, "I'm Haley."

"Michelle," she replies. "And that's my husband, Tom."

I offer Haley my hand, and when she takes it, she gives me the firmest handshake I've ever had in my life.

"Nice to meet you," she says, holding my eyes for a moment before looking back to Michelle. "This is my husband, Nathan."

Nathan nods, giving me a smile. I've only just met him, but I can tell he's shy and probably soft-spoken around his friends. Haley's the opposite, her extroverted energy radiating off of her even as she sits quietly and waits for Ryan to say something.

When we all look at him, following Haley's lead, he says, "Haley and Nathan are our biggest investors. If it weren't for them, FamFirst wouldn't exist."

"That's a lie," Haley says, rolling her eyes. "Ryan's smart. He would have figured this out without us."

"Haley flatters me," he says, giving her a warm smile before returning his attention to me. "Sorry I didn't tell you what this was all about before you got here. This isn't a business meeting or anything. I just wanted to thank you for all the hard work."

It takes me a few seconds to process what he means. I was right to think it felt like we were walking into a double date tonight. That's what's going on here.

"You invited us here to hang out with you?" I say slowly,

sure I'm right, but worried there might be something I don't know about. "Or am I missing something?"

"Yeah, basically," Andrea says, grabbing her wine glass from the table.

"And you get to expense it," Nathan says, his voice deeper than I expected.

I laugh and shake my head. "You know, I can't say I haven't done the same thing."

"One of the many perks of owning a business," he replies. "What're you drinking?"

"I don't know," I say, turning toward Michelle. "What're you getting, honey?"

Michelle chews on her lip, glancing at Andrea's wine glass before looking down at the menu and muttering, "Probably just water."

"You're not drinking?" Andrea asks, sounding like she's taking this information as a personal offense.

"My stomach has been feeling off," she says dismissively. "It must be something I ate."

"Boo!" Andrea cries. "Does this mean you're not coming out with us?"

"Not this time, no," Michelle says apologetically. We're actually going to see my friend after dinner."

"That's a bummer," Andrea says.

At the same time, Ryan says, "That sounds like a fun evening."

"I'm looking forward to it," I say, putting my hand on Michelle's knee. "I haven't seen Pippa since our wedding."

It's a lie. I've never met Pippa, and I'm not even going to meet her tonight. After this, I'll be going up to our room, and Pippa and Michelle will be catching some rom-com at the theater by Pippa's apartment. These guys don't need to know that, though.

Our conversation comes to a halt when our server appears. Michelle, true to her word, orders a water. I get the wine Andrea recommends, and Ryan orders a few appetizers for the table. We order our entrees when the server gets back with our drinks, and then Ryan levels me with a mischievous look.

"When *did* you guys get married, anyway?" he says.

We've been found out.

I scramble to come up with a date and a story, but I come up blank. Thankfully, Michelle is talking, unshaken by the question.

"August seventh of last year. The ceremony was on my aunt's property in Austin."

"You *do* strike me as a summer wedding girl," Andrea says to Michelle. Then, she says, "You, not so much."

"I'd have rather had a fall wedding," I admit, settling into character. "But the wedding was *her* day. So I just put on extra deodorant, and I was fine."

"Gross," Michelle says, scrunching her nose.

"You didn't think it was that gross when the reception was over," I reply, grinning when the entire table laughs at my joke.

Even if they had us figured out, I'm pretty sure the two of us did a pretty good job of distracting them. I'll have to remember to thank Michelle for being so fast with the wedding date. I commit it to memory just in case it comes up again.

The rest of the dinner proceeds without another hiccup. I learn that Jason was my best man (a fact I'll have to remember to fill him in on later) and that Michelle wouldn't let fondant anywhere near our wedding cake. Apparently, our wedding was the party of the summer; I'm kind of sad to have missed it.

I'm even sadder to say goodbye to Michelle when she leaves our hotel room later that night. At some point during dinner, Pippa asked Michelle to stay with her. I don't blame Michelle, but I can't help but feel a little disappointed that we're not going to have a repeat of last time.

After confirming Pippa's address where I'll be picking Michelle up tomorrow morning, I insist on ordering her an Uber. She argued that Pippa was already planning on sending one, but I make sure she knows that this is part of my apology to her friend for keeping Michelle to myself almost two months ago.

Our room is quiet without her in it, decidedly empty even though she doesn't take up that much space. It's weird the way her presence feels so right; there's something easy about spending time with her. I like when we're putting on a show for everyone, but I also really like being around her. She's quick-witted and smart as hell, too.

Michelle's exactly the kind of woman I'd like to be with, I think as I flick through the cable channels. I've known that since she helped me out the first time. I should probably ask her out on a real date.

I hit the porn channels, fully intending on surfing right through, but something stops me and sends a rush of blood below my belt. It's a POV video of a woman that looks so similar to Michelle I have to shift closer.

Her eyes are brown, not stormy blue like Michelle's. Still, their faces are similar; their noses are the exact same. Against my better judgment, I put the remote on the nightstand and give the video my full attention.

They're well past the cheesy porn dialogue and the breathing from the guy holding the camera is almost as loud as the obscene slurping noises. It's clearly fake, but with how

MY BILLIONAIRE FAKE HUSBAND

pent up I am and the models resemblance to Michelle, I'm fully hard after a few minutes.

I think about turning the TV off and going to bed, but my horny brain wins out. I push my sweats and boxers down just far enough that my cock is exposed. Then, I wrap my hand around myself, shivering at the sensation.

I'm not going to last long, not with the model that looks so much like Michelle deepthroating a massive cock on the screen in front of me. It's not difficult to imagine myself and Michelle in a similar position.

My hips cant forward as I start to stroke myself quickly, pretending my hand is her mouth, wet and warm and irresistible. I think she'd be good at this; she certainly didn't seem inexperienced when we slept together. I stopped thinking inexperience was hot a long time ago.

I slide my thumb over the head of my dick, spreading the precome collecting there down my length. I groan, not caring how loud I am. This is a hotel, after all. Can't you essentially do whatever you want in here?

I close my eyes, imagining the noises onscreen are coming from Michelle and not a porn star. My climax approaches even faster, the idea of another heated moment between us driving me insane. It's like I can't move my hand fast enough, need clouding my mind.

My heels dig firmly into the bed as I buck up into my fist harder. I bite my bottom lip so hard I'm sure I'm going to draw blood when Imaginary Michelle gags on my cock. Another couple strokes and I'm there, coming all over my hand and my shirt.

I lie there silently catching my breath, wishing Michelle were here. Eventually, the sound of the dirty movie starts to gross me out, so I turn it off and get out of bed to clean myself off.

CHAPTER 11
Michelle

I can't stop throwing up.

That's a lie. I don't throw up all the time, but I do at least once a day. That, my *super* late period, and my recent visit with Pippa led me to the family planning aisle in the drug store three blocks from my apartment.

Rows of pregnancy tests stare back at me, some boasting results two weeks sooner than others. I won't need anything fancy like that; I'm late enough that any of these should work. Somehow, that makes this harder; there are too many options, and I'm already overwhelmed by this entire situation.

The possibility of being pregnant is terrifying. Babies cost money, money I don't have. Finances have always been a source of major anxiety for me, and I'm finally starting to get my footing. A baby will ruin all of that. Also, a baby would mean moving back in with my mom in her tiny two-bedroom house so I could feed the thing.

"I always use this one," says a woman about four inches shorter than me with a toddler on her hip. She grabs a pink box and shakes it lightly in my direction. "This is what my mom used, too."

"Huh," I mutter, reeling from my interrupted anxiety spiral. I reach forward and grab the same one robotically. "That reliable?"

She shrugs. "Nothing as reliable as a doctor, but as far as at-home tests go, I know plenty of women that swear by these."

"I'll have to take your word for it," I say, still unmoving. Then, when she stays next to me, I mutter, "Thanks."

She hovers there, and I'm dreading whatever she's about to say next. I don't want advice or reassurance. I want to be anywhere but here.

"Good luck either way."

Then she walks away, the child in her arms turning to watch me as she's being carted down the aisle. Her little arm raises, her round palm opening and closing as she smiles widely. My heart clenches. I smile back at her, tears pricking behind my eyes, and I wave back. When she screams in delight, her mom turns around, giving me a curious look before disappearing.

The whole interaction leaves me with a weird feeling in my stomach, not the kind that means I'm about to be sick again. Instead, there's an undeserved sense of calm there, telling me this is going to be okay. Of course, I hope that means I'm going to start my period before I even get the chance to take this thing.

I plan on going through self-checkout to avoid any other human interaction, but luck isn't on my side when I get there. The line is long, and I only stand in it for about two minutes before the person behind me taps on my shoulder and points at the cashier with an empty line. And, because I'm distracted and not really thinking, I go.

I'm not looking forward to the conversation I'm going to have with the young boy working the register, but he's completely uninterested in what I'm buying. He only asks me if I'm paying with cash or a card. After I pay, I decline a bag and shove the test in my purse along with the receipt he hands me.

I don't really remember much of the walk home, the little pink box making my bag unthinkably heavy. When I get home, I toss it onto the counter and look at it with disdain. In my apartment, the package looks sinister, almost like a threat.

I was planning on taking it as soon as I got home, but now that I'm here, I don't know if that's such a good idea. While it could relieve a lot of stress, I've been dealing with; there's also a possibility that the test will return positive, which would worsen my stress significantly. So waiting until after I get off work tonight is probably the best idea.

It still eats at me the entire time I get ready. I almost take it right before I walk out the door, thinking it might be a good idea to have it waiting for me, but I realize how distracted I'll be and think better of it.

The walk to Metro clears my head for the most part, and once my section starts to fill up, I don't have time to think about my missed period or the pregnancy test; I'm just so busy. In fact, it floats blissfully into the back of my mind as I become the best goddamn bottle girl any of my tables have ever had.

Unfortunately, as soon as I spot Tom in my section, the entire facade comes crashing down. I'm faced with the reality of my situation and don't have time to recover before I'm greeting his table with an uncomfortable, forced smile. And when I make eye contact with him, I can tell he knows something's wrong.

I'm able to avoid that conversation for most of the night. We're busy enough that downtime is practically nonexistent; when I do manage to grab time for myself, it doesn't look like

I'm avoiding him on purpose. That is until I check my phone to find a message from Tom asking if I'll come over and talk when I find a minute.

I think about pretending I didn't see the text. He's probably going to ask why I've been acting so weird, and I have no idea what to tell him. Avoiding the conversation would be easiest for me, but that wouldn't be fair to Tom. He's just trying to be nice. But I can't tell him why I'm worried, especially since I'm probably not even pregnant. I don't know that I'd tell him even if I was.

So, I shove my phone back into its hiding place and leave the computer alcove, nearly colliding with the very person I'm trying to avoid. Tom grabs onto my elbows, keeping me from stumbling backward and falling onto my ass.

"Hey," Tom says, just loud enough for me to hear him over the music. "Everything okay?"

"Yeah," I start, taken by just how concerned he sounds. "I just, uh. I–"

"I can't hear you," he says, cutting me off. "Come on."

Then, he lets go of me and starts to walk away, glancing over his shoulder to make sure I'm following. He leads me to the hallway with the manager's office and the storage closet. I watch as he tries the knob to the storage closet.

"You need a key," I say.

"What about this one?" Tom asks, gesturing toward the other door.

"Should need a key for that one, too," I reply, watching as he shoves his shoulder against it, revealing the office inside.

"Doesn't look like we needed one," he says, stepping inside.

I follow him, closing the door behind me. "I said you *should* need one. It must have been propped open."

The way he laughs relaxes me a little. I'll be able to make

it through this; he doesn't need to know the details, anyway. I'll just tell him I have a lot going on and assure him I'm going to be okay. Easy.

"So," he says, picking his next words carefully, "everything okay? You seem a little distracted."

"I'm not distracted," I lie, immediately defensive. "My head hurts a little."

I cringe inwardly. If he hadn't called me out for being distracted, I would have stuck with my original plan; but he went straight for the jugular with this one. If I give a vague answer, that will mean admitting I am distracted. It would give him a reason to pry further.

"That must blow," he says, sliding open one of the desk drawers. "There's gotta be ibuprofen in here somewhere."

I almost ask why, then remember I'm supposed to have a headache. God, he's right. I am distracted.

"Well, that's one way to cure a headache," Tom says, smirking as he swipes something from the desk.

"What's that?"

He wags a foil packet at me playfully, but the look on his face is suggestive. He's asking a question with a wave of a condom and a quirk of his mouth.

I know I should say no, remind him I'm at work, but what comes out of my mouth is, "We have to be quick."

He hesitates, apparently not expecting me to answer like that, before dropping the condom onto the desk and surging forward to pull me into a kiss. Surprised at his enthusiasm, I do my best to keep up.

Tom tastes faintly of the Jack and Coke he was drinking at the table; the kiss is intoxicating. I grab onto him, trying to anchor myself in the moment. He's taking my request for quickness seriously, and it makes the blood rush to my head.

He presses his body close to mine; he's already starting to

get hard. I push in closer, craving the contact. That earns me a satisfied growl as he licks into my mouth and moves his hands to grab my ass. Then, he grabs the hem of my black dress and hikes it up, exposing my thong.

"You're beautiful," he tells me, kissing my cheek and nipping at my jaw. Then there's a finger against the thin fabric and mutters, "Already wet for me, huh?"

"Yeah," I whine as he rubs a circle against my clit. Through my panties, it's more antagonizing than pleasurable.

I grind down on his hand, hoping he gets the hint. He does, pulling aside the fabric and slowly pressing two fingers inside me. After giving me a couple of seconds to adjust, he starts thrusting them in and out of me.

"You ready for my cock," he asks against my lips. I whimper, nodding in response, but it must not be good enough because he says, "What was that, sweetheart?"

"I'm ready for your cock," I mutter, my words thick with lust after I realize that's what he's waiting for.

"Good girl," he says, removing his hand and leaving me feeling empty.

I don't have any room to protest, though. He's reaching behind him to grab the condom and trying to unbuckle his belt with the other. I decide to help him out, opening the front of his pants and pulling his hard length from his underwear. He rolls the condom on, and then, with strength, I didn't know he had, he hoists me into the air.

As he adjusts his grip on me, I wrap my legs around him. With the additional support, Tom's able to lift me up and then slam me back down onto his cock. He hits deep, drilling into my sweet spot. All I can do is hold on tight and let him fuck me.

I don't realize he's walking us toward the wall until my back hits it. With the additional leverage, his thrusts are ruthless. I dig my nails so hard into his back; I'm sure he can feel it through his thin shirt.

"I wish I could take my time with you," Tom pants. "You're all I can think about."

I don't know if he means that or if it's a heat-of-the-moment thing, but either way, it intensifies my fast-approaching orgasm. My toes start curling, and I'm *right there* when I hear keys rattling in the door.

Tom hears them, too, dropping me and shoving himself, condom and all, back into his pants. I scramble to get my dress back pulled down, and when I look up after I put myself back together, Tom's opening the door to reveal Jake.

"Is there a reason you two are in here?" he asks, looking between Tom and me. I can tell the question's directed at me.

I can't answer; the shock of being walked in on is too great. Tom comes to my rescue, though.

"We were talking business in the hallway," he says easily, not betraying what we were just doing to my boss. "Got a little too loud, so we ducked in here."

"You should have needed a key," Jake replies.

"That's what I said," I chime in, having found my voice.

"Okay, well," Jake says, "in the future, you're not supposed to be in here."

"Of course," I say, surprised he's letting us off this easy. "I should get back to work."

"You should," he agrees, stepping out of the doorway to let us through.

We walk out together, giggling all the way back to his table like teenagers. The rest of my shift goes by quickly. I'm still anxious about the test at home, but my encounter with Tom makes me optimistic. I'm probably not pregnant, but if I am, maybe I'll tell him. Maybe, after I take the test and sort myself out, I'll ask him about going on a real date.

By the time I get home, I'm not afraid of the pink box waiting for me on the counter. In fact, I take it as soon as I slip out of my heels. Then I change into my pajamas, queue up an episode of *Supernatural*, and heat up my leftover Chinese food from yesterday. I get my plate from the microwave and drop it on my coffee table. I sit down and am about to press play on the episode when I remember the test in my bathroom.

The nerves are suddenly back, but I figure it's best to go look at it now. It's like ripping off a bandaid. When I get to my bathroom, I hesitate, knowing what's going to be there before I even look at it. I'm still holding out hope, though.

I pick the test up by its white plastic handle and look down at the result window. Two little blue lines confirm my worst fear. I'm pregnant

CHAPTER 12
Tom

Michelle hasn't responded to my messages in five days, and I'm worried it's my fault. I was so sure that after our interrupted rendezvous that we would at least talk about what's been going on between us. But so far, she's ignored the message I sent asking if I could take her out for dinner and the various funny videos forwarded to her. I'm starting to get worried.

I'm actually so worried that I've booked myself a table at Metro alone tonight to try to talk to her. Although, now that I'm getting ready, it's dawning on me that showing up there alone might be a little creepy. I justify it by telling myself I'll be leaving an enormous tip and respecting whatever decision she makes.

I think I look well put-together, my face clean-shaven and my hair neatly styled. I'm wearing my favorite red button-down with the sleeves rolled halfway up my forearms. The black slacks I'm wearing have earned me more than a couple of compliments on my ass.

I can't remember the last time I cared this much about how I looked, but impressing Michelle is my top priority tonight. Of course, if I want to do that, I have to look the part. And smell it, too, I think as I spritz on my Armani cologne.

I'm tempted to leave early and beat the Thursday night crowd, but I don't want to look desperate. So I wait until the sun goes down and have a couple of drinks at home before I call a ride to Metro. Then, when I get there, I let myself be led to my usual table without chatting too much with the woman taking me up the stairs.

I've never been the only person at a table up here. Usually, I'm not even the first person to get here, so this is brand new. It's a little lonely, truth be told, and I find myself wishing I'd invited someone else to come along with me.

I didn't ask Victor or Eddie to come out because I'm embarrassed to tell them that I've gone and caught feelings for Michelle. I don't think they'd let me hear the end of it.

I spot Michelle before she sees me. She's talking to one of her coworkers seriously, her mouth moving fast. I can't tell from this far away, but she looks like she might be upset. But then, she makes eye contact with me and is *definitely* upset.

Coming here was definitely the wrong move. I debate getting up, running away, and calling later to leave her a tip and a hefty apology for bothering her at work. But she starts walking toward me, putting on a customer service mask.

By the time she gets to my table, though, it's morphed into something a little warmer. It's not quite the look she usually gives me, but it seems genuine.

"I wasn't expecting you tonight," she says, the smile on her face so sweet that I wish I could kiss it to get a taste.

"I know," I reply, ready to give my rehearsed answer to her unspoken question. "I had a free night and thought I'd rather drink alone here than at home."

"You know you're not alone here," Michelle says, gesturing to the full tables on either side of me.

"Are you suggesting I join strangers?" I ask teasingly. "I don't think they want you to bother them."

"Well, I'll stop in and say hi," she promises. "What're you drinking?"

"Whatever sparkling wine is your favorite."

"It'll take two bottles for you to hit the table minimum," she says. "That okay?"

"I'll share what I don't drink with my friends," I reply, nodding at the table to my right.

She laughs halfheartedly and assures me she'll be back with my first bottle, tapping the table twice before hustling away. I watch her get swallowed by the crowd, a feeling I can't quite place festering in my stomach.

The interaction didn't feel forced, but it didn't feel relaxed or casual like our conversations usually do. It's like there's a wall between us or maybe a window. We see each other, but an unseen barrier stops us from interacting normally.

When I see her again, she's got that same troubled expression on her face. It's almost identical to the look she was wearing on Saturday when I pulled her aside to talk. So maybe whatever was going on then isn't resolved yet.

"Do you want the details?" Michelle asks when she gets to my table, effortlessly opening the bottle of wine.

I can tell her heart's not in it, so I say, "No, I can read the bottle if I really need them. I trust your pallet."

She gives me a smile that says, "Thank you," and she's gone again.

While she flits around the club, I sip on the wine she dropped off. It's a red blend, a little on the dry side, not something I'd usually order, but it's nice. It reminds me of her with its earthiness and unexpected sweetness.

The next time she drops by my table, it's only long enough to see if I'm ready for my second bottle. When I tell her I'm still working on my first, she weaves through scattered groups of people to stop at a table that I know isn't in her section. One of her coworkers sidles up beside her, blocking the woman at the table from my view. I'm fairly certain she's a regular, though.

I wish I knew what they were talking about, especially because Michelle's coworker keeps throwing glances at me over her shoulder. The desire to walk by to try and grab a piece of the conversation is strong, but I think better of it. If they're talking about me, they're not going to say anything while I'm in earshot.

Actually, I should probably stop staring before they realize I've been watching them, so I pull out my phone and start scrolling through social media. It seems like all of my friends are having kids. I guess I should expect it; I am thirty-six, after all. I wasn't this surprised when they all started getting married. Kids are more permanent; if you don't like the person you married, you can just get a divorce. I can't say the same for kids.

That isn't to say I don't like kids. On the contrary, I've always wanted to be a father, but that's still a long way off. I don't even have a girlfriend; ideally, I'd like to be married before starting a family. Call me traditional if you must.

I think I'd be a good dad, though. Or, at the very least, I'd be better than my old man. He was never really around, and when he was, he wasn't interested in me. Now that I'm older, I'm pretty sure he only ever came around to eat dinner and have sex with my mom.

I was either an accident or a failed attempt to keep my dad from cheating on my mom; I never did quite get the story straight. But, whatever I was, I felt it. I was an unwelcome presence in a place I didn't ask to be. No child should have to feel like that.

"Looks like you're getting low," Michelle says, the conversation about me apparently over. She's holding another bottle of wine.

"Huh," I mutter, looking at my first nearly-empty bottle. I didn't realize I'd been drinking while I was scrolling. "Thanks."

"Of course," she says, turning like she's about to retreat.

"Has everything been okay recently?" I blurt without thinking.

"Uh," she says, revealing a chink in her armor. "It's nothing. Just some personal stuff."

"Could I take you out to get your mind off of it?"

Again, my mouth is moving before I'm cognizant of what I'm saying. I must be drunk. I probably shouldn't have any of the fresh bottle; otherwise, who knows what I'm going to say to her?

"Maybe," she says noncommittally. "I have some stuff I have to sort out."

That answer is a no if I've ever heard one. It also leaves no room for trying to convince her, which is something my drunk mind suggests I try. But I told myself I'd accept her answer, no matter what.

"Alright," I say, focusing my attention on my glass and the way the blood-red liquid splashes up the sides. "If you change your mind, you have my number."

"Thanks, Tom," she says, her voice warm. "You're really sweet."

I'm thankful for how quickly she steps away. I'm ashamed of myself for asking her out when she was upset and for being the reason she's so upset, even though I don't know what I did.

I finish the glass of wine, and when I see Michelle again, I hand her my credit card. I get the check and leave her a $200 tip. On my way out, I hand off my leftover alcohol to a table of cute girls, waiting until I'm on the sidewalk to order a ride.

While I wait for Daisy in a white Kia Soul to pick me up, I run through the entirety of my relationship with Michelle. And, when she gets here, I'm sure I know where I fucked up.

I shouldn't have asked her for sex a few days ago. It was wrong of me to do that while she was upset. Even worse, she could have gotten in trouble with her boss. There's no way he bought my lie. Jake's not an idiot.

When I get home, I've moved on to brainstorming ways to make it up to her. I've never wanted to be back on someone's good side so badly. Hopefully, I haven't completely trashed things between the two of us.

CHAPTER 13
Michelle

My life, at least as I know it, is over. I've been trying to pretend things are normal, especially at work, but Tom keeps showing up. It's not like he's being creepy or anything. On the contrary, I think his presence would be comforting if it weren't for the fact that I haven't told him I'm pregnant, but because I haven't, seeing him just fills me with a bloodcurdling sense of guilt.

I know I should tell him, but every time I think about it, I feel like I'm going to get in trouble. Yes, it takes two people to make a baby, but I'm the one who said we'd be fine without a condom. I'm the one that forgot to take my birth control. I'm the one who started everything.

God, I haven't even put any thought into what I'm going to do. The only people I've told besides Pippa are Rue, one of my coworkers, and Amber, one of Rue's regulars. And I only clued them in because Amber could tell something was up between Tom and me.

That was an embarrassing conversation. I didn't tell them everything, just that he and I hooked up, and now I'm pregnant. Amber's questions weren't too invasive, but they made me squirm.

How did I know the baby was his? *Well, he's the only person I've slept with in a while.* What? Really? You're too pretty not to be getting laid all the time. *I know, Amber. I'm just so busy all the time.* That's a damn shame. Rue, honey, stop looking at him.

Anyway, I'm sure Tom knows we were talking about him. I think that might be why he keeps showing up and leaving me big tips.

"Are you seriously complaining about him giving you money right now?" Pippa asks.

She keeps calling to check up on me, and I get it. If she were in my situation, I'd do the same thing, but it's a little suffocating. I feel like I haven't had any time to think about this on my own.

"I'm not complaining about the money," I reply. "I'm complaining about how him giving me the money makes me feel."

"You're at work. He's tipping you for your service," she says logically, ever the voice of reason when shit hits the fan. "It shouldn't make you feel any sort of way, especially when you *need* the money."

"Okay, but he left me $500 two nights ago," I shoot back because she has to understand that accepting such large amounts of money feels like charity to me. "That's a lot of money, Pips."

"Then it sounds like you provided him with some damn good service," she says, adjusting her neck pillow; she's got another hour before her flight home boards.

"But still," I say, the words falling flat because I don't really have an argument that doesn't sound stupid.

Pippa chews on the inside of her cheek thoughtfully. She's

probably close to understanding what I'm getting at; we've never really needed words to know what the other is thinking. After a few seconds, she nods.

"What would make you feel better about him giving you that money?"

"Him not giving me the money," I say honestly.

"Okay," she says, a little exasperated. "From what I can tell, this guy doesn't mind giving you money. Honestly, he acts like he *likes* giving you money."

"Please don't say that," I reply. "That makes me feel like a prostitute."

"Not a prostitute," Pippa says. "I think Tom actually cares about you. You're more like a sugar baby if you're going to label it."

"That's absolutely not what this is," I say.

"So you agree that all the money he gives you is for the work you're doing and not because of your relationship?" she asks, a smarmy grin on her face.

"Oh, fuck you," I say. "I'm allowed to feel guilty about this. He'll probably hate me when he finds out."

The sigh she lets out is long-suffering, and I'm pretty sure her eyes roll into the back of her head. Then, she says, "I doubt he's going to hate you. Maybe he'll be freaked out, but I don't think he's going to hate you. He is the one that got you pregnant, after all."

"But–"

"It's not all your fault, Michelle," she snaps, shutting me right up. "It was a group effort."

"Yeah," I say, dejected. "I know."

"I think you should tell him," she says. "He could probably help you figure everything out so you can stay in Austin."

"Yeah…" I reply, knowing she's right. Any further protest

would just be stupid, and I need to start working up the courage to tell him.

"Or," she continues, "you could always just drop your whole life there and come live with me in my extra bedroom. I've been here long enough that I could twist an arm or two and get us into the next available three-bedroom."

"I couldn't ask you to do that."

"You're not asking," she reminds me. "I'm offering. You keep talking about losing your apartment and having to move back with your mom because babies are expensive. I don't want that to happen to you, *and* I want unrestricted access to my niece or nephew. If you're not going to let the rich guy help you, ditch Austin and come to Houston."

That's tempting. So tempting that I almost tell her so, but I don't want to get Pippa's hopes up, nor do I want her to try to convince me, so I give her an uninterested "Maybe," in response.

She hums, seemingly out of things to say. Then, finally, she mutters, "You gonna be okay if I hop off of here to grab something to eat?"

"Yeah," I promise, secretly glad I won't be sitting on the phone with her for another fifty minutes. "Let me know when you land?"

"I will," she says. "I love you, Michelle. If you need me before my flight leaves, just give me a call, okay? I have my ringer on for you."

"I love you, too," I say, hoping she can feel how much I mean it through the phone.

She makes me hang up like she's worried that if she's the one to end the call, she'll upset me. When my screen goes dark, I groan and look up at my ceiling. There's so much I should be doing, but I'm overwhelmed by the sheer enormity of it all.

Pippa's solutions, while helpful, circle back to acknowledging that I'm with child and making a lifestyle change accordingly. We already discussed going to a clinic, but I don't think I could follow through with that. Right now, I think I want to marinate in denial; then, I'll figure out what I'm going to do.

Moving in with Pippa is my most appealing option, especially if I do as she suggests and just leave with no explanation. I've actually always fantasized about running away and starting a new life somewhere else, but I've never had an excuse to do it until now.

I let myself think about it for a moment. I'd miss this apartment the most, I think. Regardless of the financial pain in the ass, this place has been, it's a symbol of all the hard work I've done my entire life. Leaving would be hard, I think. Not only do I have almost two years of mostly good memories here, but I also have an excessive amount of stuff; art hanging on the walls, decorative knick-knacks, and piles of mail on the kitchen island and coffee table.

And, if I stay with Pippa, I'll be in the heart of downtown Houston. Sure, it's not the same as Austin, but I think I could learn to like it. I've never had a bad time there, and I'm sure I could carve out a place for myself there the same way I carved one out here before I started working all the time.

If I leave, I'll miss my coworkers and the few friends I have that still check in on me. I'll miss Tom. *Fuck*. I'll miss Tom.

That hits me like a train. I like him. I actually genuinely like him. If I weren't pregnant, I'd be trying to make him my boyfriend. But if I were to try anything now, it would look like I got pregnant on purpose to make him stick around. That's absolutely not what I want. I want him to be interested in me for *me*, not because we have a kid together.

There's no way I can tell him. It would complicate our whole relationship. He might do something stupid like commit himself to me now and then realize years down the line that he doesn't want me. Everyone wants to be a parent until they realize how much work it actually is. He'd probably be miserable.

Actually, if I keep this from him, I'm doing him a favor. I won't go after child support; I'll just let him live his life blissfully unaware. He can keep having fun and living it up as a bachelor without the responsibility of a baby he didn't ask for.

Maybe I can look him up in a few years, and we can try again. Then, he doesn't have to know the kid is his; if something happens between us, he'll be choosing fatherhood instead of having it thrust upon him.

Convinced that I've come to the best decision for everyone, I unpause my show and dissociate until Netflix pauses the show to ask if I'm still here. I figure another three episodes won't hurt, so I select the "Still Watching" option, but I start to drift off about halfway through the second episode and dream of fields of bluebells.

CHAPTER 14
Tom

I thought that after our interrupted rendezvous, Michelle and I would talk about what's been going on between us. I was sure we had a deeper connection and mutual interest, but she barely responds to my messages anymore, even after I talked to her at work a couple of weeks ago.

I've shown up a couple more times, even though I know I probably shouldn't. After my first visit, I convinced myself I was making up the way her face fell when she looked at me, but now, I'm starting to think I really am part of the problem. Still, I leave her increasingly larger tips in a lame attempt at a wordless apology.

I've thought about asking her to dinner or even calling her and asking if she has a minute to talk, but it's clear that she's not interested in hearing from me. I can tell when I'm not wanted, so I've thrown myself into work to distract myself from the sharp sting of rejection.

Honestly, even if I weren't trying to occupy all my spare time, FamFirst would still be getting it anyway. We're two weeks from the launch and keep finding bugs. It's little things, mislabeled buttons, and glitches on some screens, but we promised to deliver a perfect product. So I've been dedicating hours of my time to the office, only leaving to sleep or see Michelle at work. I've even been getting all of my meals that I don't have at Metro delivered.

Maybe it's a little excessive, but I want to impress Ryan and his team. He's been helping all he can, sending in bug reports for things that slipped through the cracks. I'm sure clients will find other things that we haven't, but this is a good start. When it goes public, app maintenance should be a breeze.

"You should go home and get some sleep," Eddy says, materializing behind me and making me jump.

"Shit, you scared me," I reply, swiveling my desk chair around to get a better look at him.

Eddy's stopped dressing up for the office, clad in joggers and a sweatshirt. A pair of headphones is slung around his neck. He seems amused at catching me off guard, but there's an exhaustion that creeps into his features.

"That's the sleep deprivation, boss," he says.

"You're probably right," I chuckle, scrubbing a hand over my face. "I'll head home once I get this done."

I can tell Eddy wants to argue with me and tell me it'll be here in the morning, but he doesn't. I'm pretty sure he's picked up on the riff between Michelle and me.

"Alright, well. I'll see you tomorrow, Tom."

"See ya, Eddy."

I get back to work as soon as he leaves the office. He's right; I need sleep, but I've finally identified the issue that's stumped everyone else in the office all day. I'm pulled out of my workflow by my work email chiming.

Normally, I'd ignore it. It's so late that the email's probably junk, but still, I open the email app, just in case. At the top of my inbox is an unread email from Ryan Gibson addressed to everyone on my team. I open it and read through the text.

FamFirst is hosting a launch party in Houston, and everyone on my team is invited with a plus one. I read through the invitation, dread making my whole body cold. There's no way I can ask Michelle to tag along.

I also don't trust that my team will be able to keep from making jokes about our relationship being fake. Although it was one thing to pretend to be married in front of strangers, it's completely different doing it in front of people we know. They know our regular dynamic and might burst into laughter if they see us kiss.

I doubt she'd even say yes. Things have been so tense between the two of us lately that I'm almost positive she doesn't want to spend any alone time with me. Plus, even if she did say yes, I don't think we'd be able to pull off the "happily married" act anymore.

This is definitely a problem for tomorrow, so I close the window and go back to my lines of code when a text message comes through on my cellphone. It's from Ryan, telling me about the email I just read and informing me Andrea can't wait to see Michelle again.

Well, shit. Michelle's been personally requested. So I've got to ask her, even though she's probably going to say no. Maybe she can help me come up with an excuse to give Ryan.

I can't muster up the courage to call her right now, so I fire off a text message with all of the details. Then, I set my phone aside and try to focus on my work. Eventually, I get back into my rhythm, and I forget all about the message.

When I finally wrap up an hour later, I don't think to check my phone. The only thing I care about is getting home and getting to bed. My alarm goes off at the same time every day, so I don't even have to bother with that.

In the morning, though, I have two missed texts and a missed call from Michelle. So I don't even bother with reading the texts, opting to return her call. While the phone rings, I realize I should have read what she had to say first, but I'm eager to hear her voice.

Although, I'm not sure I'm actually going to get to talk to her. The ringing goes on for so long that I start to rehearse the message I'm going to leave, but then there's a click on the other end, and Michelle says, "Hello?"

The background sounds busy like she's in public. I can hear dishes clattering against each other and maybe someone yelling. I definitely should have checked those messages.

"It's a little loud on your end. Is now a bad time?" I ask.

"Kind of," she replies. "I'm at work."

"Work?" I say. "I didn't know Metro was open this early."

"It's not," she says, her voice barely audible over the noise. "I work at Peggy's most weekdays."

"No shit?" I say, amazed that she handles two jobs with such grace. "I can let you go. Do you have time to talk later?"

"I should be out of here by three. I'll call you then," she says quickly, hanging up without saying goodbye.

With the phone call over, I belatedly read the text messages containing the same information she gave me. I feel like an asshole for not checking them first; she probably thinks I was trying to demand her attention or something.

I really need to watch myself around her. Clearly, there's something going on that I'm not privy to. Even if I've blown any chance I've had to be with her romantically, I want to be supportive. That means pushing my own feelings aside and prioritizing hers.

That's not so hard when I get to work. Victor immediately pulls me to his computer with a problem he's been having all morning as soon as I cross the threshold. I don't get to my desk until about an hour later.

The first thing I do when I settle into my chair is check my email. Waiting for me, still selected from last night, is the invitation from Ryan I haven't responded to. I haven't replied to his text, either. I should do something about it now that the workday has started.

After a little deliberation, I shoot off a message to Ryan to let him know we're waiting to see if Michelle's able to take the night off of work. I can't believe I didn't think to use her job as an excuse last night. If she says no, I've got a rock-solid excuse. I might actually offer it to her when we talk later.

I want her to come, though, so I'm not going to offer it right off the bat.

Ryan texts back almost immediately with a fingers-crossed emoji. I smile down at it, wishing I was still living in a world where I could pretend Michelle and I are together. I'm not a fan of how different things feel now that I know there's no possibility for more. It's not a game anymore; it's just a business transaction.

I shove that thought to the back of my mind just in time for another bug report to pop into my inbox. That keeps me busy well past my normal lunchtime. I'm in my car, scarfing down a burrito, when my phone starts ringing.

When I realize it's Michelle, I almost choke on the mouthful of beans, cheese, and steak. I take a few long gulps of my drink to clear my throat before swiping to answer the call.

"Michelle, hey," I say quickly.

"Hi, Tom," she replies, sounding exhausted. "So what're the details of this thing?"

Straight to business, I can respect that.

"The new, redesigned FamFirst app is launching in a little less than two weeks," I say, wiping sour cream away from the corner of my mouth. "Sorry, I can't remember the exact date right now. Looks like it's dinner and drinks, nothing intense. As always, I'd pay you."

She's so quiet that I worry there's something wrong with our connection, but finally, she says, "I don't know…"

"I can pay you $4,000," I say, knowing that's way more than I should offer. Maybe it's wrong, maybe it's desperate, but I want her there.

"I–" Michelle starts, cutting herself off. It's almost like I can hear the cogs in her brain turning, and eventually, she chokes out, "Did you say $4,000?"

"Yeah," I reply as I squeeze my eyes shut and cringe at the amount of money I'm offering her. Still, I press on. "It should be the last time we have to do this, too."

"Okay," she says after another tense, unbearable pause. "Okay, I'll do it."

I want to ask her if she's sure and offer to cover for her because it's clear she doesn't want to come, but I think she might *really* need the money.

"I'll send you all the details," I tell her. "I've got to get off of here so I can get back to work."

"Alright," she replies. "I'll see you soon."

She hangs up before I return the sentiment, so I end up telling my empty car goodbye. I don't finish my lunch, my stomach in knots because I'm paying Michelle so much money to hang out with me. And, even worse, there's a flutter of excitement at the prospect of seeing her and pretending to be her husband again.

Thank God work's here to distract me.

CHAPTER 15
Michelle

Saying yes to attending this thing was a mistake, no matter how much money Tom's giving me. I feel gross; my head hurts a little, I'm having these terrible cramps, and I just want a drink. On the plus side, Andrea has told me I'm glowing. Although, the way she said it made it sound a lot like she *knows*.

I received a thorough ribbing from Victor, Eddy, and Angela for not visiting the open bar while we were mingling earlier. Now that we're all sitting at a table in a conference room that's been converted for this launch party, I'm sipping from my water with the glass of red wine I ordered to keep them from asking why I'm not drinking.

I've read somewhere that you can have a glass of red wine a day while you're pregnant, so if I sip from the one in front of me for the rest of the night, I can keep everyone here happy.

The caterers are coming by to pick up our salad dishes now, and I can see a fresh wave of them coming into the room with our main dishes. They're dropping things off starting at the back of the room, and our table is close to the front, so

Ryan can stand and give his presentation about the app when dinner's finished.

"Do you remember what you ordered?" Andrea asks, knocking her elbow against me.

She's been putting all of her efforts into getting me into a better mood tonight. It's sweet, but I wish I could tell her to stop, that I've been lying to her about my relationship with Tom. My budding friendship with her makes this whole thing feel even more disingenuous now, not that it had ever been genuine, to begin with. Tom and I just took the game we were playing way too far.

"No," I say, doing my best to get myself back into the conversation. "Um. Tom filled out the RSVP, I think."

"Did you really not ask your wife what she wanted for dinner, Tom?" she asks, trying to force some playfulness into the conversation.

"I got the salmon and the steak," he replies with a shrug, taking a sip from his Old Fashion. "I sent in the RSVP while she was working. Which one do you want, Michelle."

I'm not sure if I can have steak that isn't well done, but I'm positive I shouldn't have fish, so I say, "You can have the salmon."

"That's what I was hoping you'd say," he replies. I think he's trying to get back to the playful banter we maintained the last two times we were with Ryan and Andrea, but it falls flat.

At least this is the last time I'm going to have to come to an event like this.

"So," Ryan says, glancing at Victor and Eddy quickly before looking back at Tom and me, "how have things been?"

"Busy," Tom says immediately, not giving me any room to say anything.

He doesn't want to be here, either. Things have been formal and tense between us since he picked me up. I was hoping that it would dissipate when we arrived, but that isn't what happened.

"I suppose that's partially my fault," Ryan says lightly, glancing at the caterers getting closer to us. Then, he looks at Andrea for help like he's been doing all night.

"What about you, Michelle," she asks, pulling the attention off of Tom. "How's work been?"

"Pretty good," I reply, relieved that I actually have something to talk about. "Our summer DJ series is wrapping up soon, so I've been helping our promoter get the word out."

"Promoter?" Andrea says. "You've been promoting?"

"I've been–"

"Steak?" a caterer asks, setting down an enormous tray stacked with plates filled with small portions of veggies, potatoes, and, I *think,* ribeyes.

It takes a few minutes to get plates in front of everyone – after the first caterer left, a second came to pass out the salmon dishes. Then, we all go silent, digging into our food. It's good, but I don't really taste too much of it.

Tom's very carefully avoiding touching me in any way, keeping his elbows tucked and his movements stiff. It really hurts, but I know it's my fault. I've kept him in the dark about what's going on. I thought it was for his own good, but maybe Pippa was right; maybe I needed to tell him about the baby.

"Do you want to be a promoter?" Ryan asks when the sound of metal against ceramic stalls.

I wash down the food in my mouth with a swig of wine before saying, "Not really. I like being a bottle girl. I was just trying to fill up my section."

Everyone at the table laughs, and the tension eases a little. Eddy starts talking about the DJ we had playing three weeks ago, and the conversation starts to flow again. I'm emboldened by the smile still lingering on Tom's face, so I reach over, resting my hand on his upper thigh.

His muscles twitch under my touch. I watch his expression carefully; confusion flits across his face, then he glances at me. I smile warmly, which he returns before jumping into the conversation to talk about how amazing the music at Metro is.

Ryan eventually stops the conversation, though, standing and making his way to the podium. It takes the crowd less than a minute to give him their full attention. I get the impression that these people really respect him.

"Hi, everyone," he says into the mic. "Thanks for coming out to join us for dinner. I'll keep this brief so we can get to dinner, and if you're interested in coming to the after-party, see my beautiful wife or me" next to me, Andrea raises her hand and waves, "and we'll let you know where we're going. I'm not sure if you guys got babysitters for tonight, but we did, and we plan on getting our money's worth."

This gets a polite chuckle from the crowd. Ryan waits until the noise dies down before continuing.

"We actually found our sitter tonight on FamFirst. She's one of the thousands of qualified caregivers on the app. We hired her confidently, knowing she passed a criminal background check. Thanks to her caregiver bio, we also know that her childcare methods align with ours.

"If you're a parent, you understand how important it is to have trust in the person you're leaving your child with. That's why I started the development of FamFirst.

"My wife and I struggled with infertility for years. But, almost two years ago, we were made the luckiest people on the planet. After countless rounds of IVF, one of the embryos took, and we were pregnant."

A round of applause goes through the room, and I think

Andrea might be crying next to me. I feel kind of bad for having such a negative reaction to finding out I'm having a baby. Some people spend years trying to make this happen.

"I was so excited that I immediately started looking into daycares, preschools, and babysitters, which I'm learning is *exactly* what you want to do. Unfortunately, if you wait until they're born, all the good ones won't have room for you. Actually, if I could do it over again, I would have started looking when we started our IVF consultations."

The crowd laughs, but my stomach sinks. Should I be looking for daycares and preschools? Am I already messing all of this up?

"If you're a parent, you also know how difficult it is to find reputable people and childcare institutions. There's no one-stop shop. So I compiled workbook after workbook on Excel with every piece of information I could find about every daycare, preschool, and nanny in Houston. That was the bones of FamFirst.

"The first iterations of the app were made specifically for my wife and me and our close family and friends. Haley Twillings, one of my wife's closest friends, was the first person to tell me I had a great product on my hands. She provided the funding while I got the business side of FamFirst set up.

"We launched that product just two months after my daughter, Stephanie, was born. Since then, the database has only gotten larger, and we've incorporated user reviews to help parents know they're making the right decision with the most precious thing in their lives.

A lot has changed, but a lot has stayed the same. Our mission is to make finding trusted caregivers easier, so we welcomed some new faces into the family, and they're here tonight. Could the guys from Bridges Solutions stand up for me? Your partners, too."

Reluctantly, I stand with Tom. He's not even looking my way. Eddy and Victor rise with their girlfriends, who look excited to be recognized. Before we can be applauded, Ryan clicks a button that changes the projector background behind him from the company logo to a screenshot of the redesigned app and keeps speaking.

"These guys are amazing at their jobs, and because of them, we're launching a product that's streamlined the process," he says proudly, smiling at Tom.

I remember I'm supposed to be acting as his wife, so I reach out to rub his arm in a supportive gesture. I'm surprised at the way he leans into the touch. Maybe I haven't lost him with my coolness. Maybe I have a chance to fix this.

"There's a massive update coming on Monday," he continues, eyes sweeping over the crowd. We all take that as our signal to be seated again. "They've added a social aspect to the app that allows parents to recommend caregivers to other parents on the app. In addition to that, the entire interface is more user-friendly. It's now easier than ever to hire a babysitter or a nanny or find the best daycare for your little one."

The clapping that comes after that statement is thunderous, and I can tell Ryan wasn't expecting it. He jumps slightly and then smiles wide. He waits for the clapping to subside before leaning back down to the microphone.

"Thanks, guys! If you want to thank these guys, buy them a drink after this," he says with childlike excitement. "I'm going to let y'all get back to dessert. Thanks again for coming out."

And with that, he steps away from the podium and comes back to the table. Tom shakes his hand and thanks him, but my brain doesn't really process any of the words—drinks after this. There's no way I'm going to be able to get out of that.

If I go and don't order anything to drink, someone might call me out. I might have to explain myself, which would be a terrible way for Tom to find out. But staying back at the hotel would raise suspicions, too.

I spend the rest of our meal picking at the chocolate cake in front of me and trying to figure out what I'm going to do. Luckily, Eddy's gone off on some tangent, so I don't have to put too much effort into making it look like I'm paying attention to the conversation.

"You feeling up to going out tonight, or do you want me to cover you?" Tom whispers in my ear.

He's looking at me so earnestly, his face full of genuine concern. Guilt licks at my sides and I tell him, "Maybe we should both stay in tonight."

He gives me a sideways glance; then, after a beat, I see realization flash across his features; he knows there's something I need to tell him. His face hardens and he nods before finishing his drink. His reaction makes me feel worse; he's like a dog that got into the trash when his owner was out. I squash down the urge to tell him everything's okay because that would be a lie; I can't even tell him that thing *will* be okay. Who knows how he's going to take the news.

Only a few minutes later, Ryan clears his throat and looks around the table expectantly, waiting for the attention of everyone else.

"How do we want to split rides?" he asks, already tapping away at his phone. "I think there are too many of us for an UberXL."

"Actually," Tom says with an anxious glance in my direction – again I'm struck by the urge to reassure him, "I think Michelle and I are going to sit this one out."

"What?!" Ryan cries, sounding personally offended at the proclamation. "Again?"

"Ryan," Andrea snaps, giving him a look that says they'll talk later. "Do you remember being taught about peer pressure in school?"

"Yes?" he says, like he isn't following her line of thought.

"You're the peer pressure they taught us about," she replies. "They don't want to come. That's okay."

Her tone allows no room for argument. She *knows*. Sure, there's no way she knows everything, but she knows I'm pregnant and knows that *very* few people have this information. I wish we weren't lying to her; it would be nice to have someone that's already had a kid in my corner on this journey.

Unfortunately for me, this situation is anything but ideal and our relationship is founded on a huge lie. I'm appreciative of Andrea's support all the same, though.

Slowly, as attendees finish their desserts, our table is surrounded. Most of them want to congratulate Ryan, but there are a few pressing for details of the afterparty. I'm starting to feel claustrophobic and anxious that someone's going to push us to come out with them again.

"You ready to get back to the hotel?" Tom asks, sensing my discomfort.

I face him, and he turns into the only person in the room, everyone and everything else just turning into background noise. From the softness of his features and intensity of his gaze, I think he might feel the same.

"Yeah," I say, my voice barely a whisper in the crowded room.

Tom stands, tells everyone we're going to leave, and

grabs my hand. I lace our fingers together as he leads me through the crowds of people clustered around the tables out of the space. When his fingers twitch in mine on the sidewalk outside, an indication he wants to drop my hand, I tighten my grip.

He holds onto me until our ride pulls up. I try to ignore how empty my hand feels when we get in the car.

CHAPTER 16
Tom

The air is charged. It has been since I picked Michelle up in front of her apartment earlier today, and now I'm on the precipice of learning why. Something about how she holds herself tells me everything's about to change. Her body is held still, and there's tension in her shoulders and jaw.

I still can't tell if it's my fault or not. She barely talked to me on the ride into Houston and disappeared into the hotel lobby to talk to Pippa when we got there. When she came back up to the room to get ready, it felt like things were looking up. Then all of that went away when we got to the event. As soon as we were around other people, she closed herself off, kind of like she's doing now.

I'm worried we'll spend the rest of the night swimming in tense silence. I know she held onto me after we left the dinner, but now it feels like she changed her mind and would rather be anywhere but here. No matter what, I will respect that she wants privacy, but I hate being left in the dark. I have a sinking feeling that something I've done is playing into her hot and cold behavior.

When we get to the hotel, Michelle gets out of the car first and rushes to get through the lobby door. I sigh and resign myself to a night of silence, accepting that she needs space and that she won't be telling me what's going on.

I'm not expecting Michelle to be waiting for me next to one of the gray leather couches. So it's even more surprising when she reaches out and takes my hand in hers. I start to feel better when our fingers interlock.

The journey up to our hotel room is quiet but a comfortable kind of quiet. The kind of quiet that says we're in this together. I hope she feels it, too, and I hope she actually tells me what's wrong. I hope she lets me give her the comfort and support she deserves.

"I'm going to take a shower," she says as I drop the "Do Not Disturb" sign on the doorknob.

I don't answer; I'm afraid to shatter this delicate atmosphere we've created. So instead, I nod and try to stay out of her way as she gathers her things and shuts herself into the bathroom. The shower is on for almost half an hour, and she comes out, her cheeks flushed and her hair damp, about twenty minutes later. I shove my nose back into my phone, not wanting her to feel watched as she packs her dirty stuff into her bag.

She settles in next to me on the foot of the bed, looking at her hands. She picks at the skin around her thumbnail, sighs, and says, "We need to talk."

Even though I knew this was coming, my stomach drops. My expression remains trained when I lock my phone and put it on the bed, screen side down. My voice only sounds slightly wrong to my ears as I force out, "Yeah, sure. What's up?"

I can't really read Michelle's expression; fear, exhaustion, and stress are there. The corners of her mouth twitch as she considers her next words. My heart beats so hard in my chest that I can feel it in my throat.

"I'm pregnant."

The words don't make sense at first. I hear them and know what they mean, but I can't get them to connect to our situation in my brain; how could those words have anything to do with us right now?

"What?" I say not so eloquently as I try to force my mind to catch up.

She laughs, but there's no humor in it, and for some reason, that's what makes everything click for me. Michelle and I had sex without a condom, and she's pregnant. That's why she's been so distant lately, so hot and cold.

"Mine?" I ask, even though I know there's no other reason she'd be telling me.

"Yeah," Michelle replies, not looking me in the eyes. "You're the only person I've slept with in, like, six months. I guess my birth control didn't work."

I nod, unable to form a single coherent thought. Instead, I'm bombarded with a tornado of emotions that tears apart every synapse of my mind. Fear is at the forefront of everything; I'm afraid of the change to my life and the change to hers. I'm afraid of what this means for us. But, most of all, I'm afraid that I'll be a bad father.

"You don't have to be involved if you don't want to," she says, apparently taking my silence as a negative reaction. "I'm okay with doing this alone."

"I want to be involved," I say, unable to have her think I'd abandon the responsibility I have to this kid.

She nods, breathing out through her mouth slowly. While she takes a moment for herself, the rest of the pieces of the puzzle click together. I wonder if she was actually expecting me to take the out she just offered. I guess plenty of guys would; I try not to be hurt by her assuming I'm one of them.

"When's your next doctor's appointment?" I ask, wanting to make it clear I'm serious. "I'll drive you and stay with you."

Then, inexplicably, her shoulders start shaking, and tears spring to her eyes. She quickly hides her face in her hands, and I act before I can think about it. I put my arm around her and pull her into my chest, burying my fingers in her hair and rubbing her back.

Michelle melts into me, wrapping her arms around my body and practically crawling onto my lap. She cries, and it seems like she hasn't let herself do this before now; my heart aches for her. I murmur that it's going to be okay and press kisses against the crown of her head.

Eventually, her shaking stops, and her breathing starts to even out. I keep my arms around her, though, and she makes no attempt to move away. We stay there, existing in each other's arms for so long that I lose track of time.

"You know everything's going to be okay, right?" I ask. Then, before she can argue, I add, "You're not going to have to do this alone, not if you don't want to."

"I don't want to," she says after a few seconds, but she doesn't sound fully convinced. She pulls away from me and says with more conviction, "I don't want to do it alone."

"Then you're not doing this alone," I say, glancing down at her lips. "We'll figure this out together, okay?"

"Okay," she replies, leaning up to kiss me.

It's tender and slow, almost like she's expecting me to push her away. Instead, I respond decisively, tightening my fingers in her hair and running my tongue along the seam of her mouth. She's receptive, opening up to let me taste her.

As we kiss, Michelle starts to straddle me properly, but I

stop her, guiding her so she's resting against the pillows at the head of the bed. Her legs fall open to accommodate me, and I'm careful to keep my quickly hardening cock from touching her too soon. I want this to be about her. I *need* this to be about her.

I hold myself above her as we make out, but eventually, I pull away, hooking my hands in the waistband of her soft sleep shorts. In response, she lifts her hips up from the bed, watching me intently as I slide them and her panties off and toss them to the floor.

Then, I lower myself between her legs with my body flush against the bed, giving my hard dick a little bit of friction. I slide my hands under her back and pull her toward me as I kiss and nip up the soft flesh of her inner thighs. She shoves a fist against her mouth to stifle the noises she's making, but that won't do.

"Let me hear you," I say into the crease between her cunt and her thigh, punctuating the statement with a particularly harsh bite.

That gives me the reaction I'm looking for a loud moan coupled with her legs tightening around my head. I let myself be pulled into her sweetness, licking a stripe with the flat of my tongue against her labia. When I get to her clit, I circle it before sucking it into my mouth slowly.

Her mouth is open, and her chest heaves as she watches me eat her out. I keep my eyes on her as I keep going, making obscene, pornographic noises that match the ones leaving her lips. My hips cant forward, grinding against the mattress without my permission. I can't help it; this is insanely hot.

"Tom," she says urgently, her hands flying to my hair. "Tom, I'm about to come."

I don't let her pull me off, opting to keep my ministrations steady and coax an orgasm out of her. Unfortunately, I don't get to hear it in all of its glory because her thighs clamp over my ears and block out most of the sound as she rides out waves of pleasure. I don't mind all that much, though. It's driving me crazy being able to feel her climax like this.

As soon as she relaxes her legs, she pulls me up to kiss me, her tongue chasing her own flavor. I groan into her mouth and press my hardness against her, asking a silent question. Michelle answers by reaching between us to unbutton my pants.

She struggles with them for a few seconds before I help out and push my slacks and boxers down past my ass, freeing my mostly-neglected cock. Then, without warning, she grabs my length and strokes me twice, her thumb rubbing over the tip and spreading pre-come down the shaft.

My body jerks forward, chasing her touch. And, when she laughs at my efforts against my lips, I can't help but take control, resting the head of my cock against her wetness. Instinctively, she tilts her hips and lets me slide in.

I only give her a few seconds to adjust before I start rolling my hips, slowly at first, before speeding up at Michelle's command. The bed squeaks beneath us as I fuck her relentlessly. I'm quickly approaching the edge, but I'm determined to give her another orgasm before I come.

"Tell me how you're doing," I say, my lips gazing at the shell of her ear as I speak.

"Good," she whines, clawing at my back through my shirt.

"Just good?" I reply, angling my hips and successfully hitting her G-spot and pulling a moan out of her.

"Gonna come again," she says, sounding delirious. "Gonna come again."

"Then come for me, sweetheart," I say, leaning down to capture her mouth in a searing kiss.

It doesn't take long for her to tense up beneath me, her body tightening around my cock as she comes for the second time tonight. I follow behind her shortly after, gasping her name and burying my face in the crook of her neck as I ride out my own high.

We're quiet for the next several minutes, breathing in each other's presence. Eventually, I have to pull out and break the silence.

"I'm serious, Michelle," I say, pulling away so I can look her in her eyes. She tries to look away, but I don't let her. "I'll be here with you every step of the way. You aren't going to do this alone."

"I know," she says, sounding unsure.

I don't know how I'm going to convince her everything's going to be okay. Truthfully, I have no idea if everything's going to be okay. Neither of us is ready to be parents, and so much could go wrong. I only know that I won't let her raise this baby alone.

CHAPTER 17
Michelle

It's probably too late to tell Tom I've changed my mind about him taking me to my ultrasound appointment, considering it starts in forty-five minutes, and he's almost to my apartment. I have time to order another ride, but I don't want to be rude.

I don't know what's wrong with me. It's like my brain refuses to accept that Tom actually means well. My dad abandoned me and my mom after sticking with her through her entire pregnancy, what's going to stop him from doing the same thing?

Logically, I know Tom is nothing like my dad. He's sweet, soft-spoken, and genuinely considerate of my feelings. He's a walking green flag. He practically jumped at the opportunity to come to this ultrasound with me. I don't think there are a lot of men willing to do that.

Still, there's a nagging voice at the back of my mind telling me that I can't trust anyone, especially not a man, to take care of me. The voice tells me I can't get reliant on him financially, that that would be a mistake. The voice sounds eerily like my mother.

My mom doesn't know I'm pregnant yet. She'll probably be the last person to know. Mom thinks I really have my shit together, so there's no way I can drop this bomb on her if I don't have some sort of solution already lined up. She definitely isn't going to accept Tom as a solution.

A phone call from Tom pulls me back into the present moment. I answer it, already knowing what he's going to say.

"I'm out front," he says instead of saying hello back.

"Cool," I say, pretending his lack of greeting doesn't upset me; I know I'm irrationally sensitive. "I'll be down in a second."

"Take your time," he says kindly before hanging up.

If I took my time, I'd never get down there. So I force myself out of my apartment and take the stairs, knowing that if I wait for the elevator, I might get cold feet.

When I get into his car, we finally exchange greetings, but we don't really talk much on the way to the obstetrician's office. I can't help but lament the fact that I picked this one on Yelp with Pippa over FaceTime instead of with the input of my mom or Tom. Not that he didn't offer; I'm just refusing his help.

I do all the talking when we get to the receptionist, but Tom stays by my side the whole time. It surprises me; I guess I was expecting him to immediately find a seat and tuck himself out of the way. But instead, he even offers to drop my paperwork back off with the receptionist – I decline because I'm not *that* pregnant.

The nerves come back in full force when we're waiting to be called back. It's not like getting a scan from the doctor makes this any more or less real, but it feels like once I go back there and have that wand shoved inside me (yes, I asked if it's going inside me, and it is), my fate will be sealed.

When a nurse calls me back, Tom stands to come back

with me. I'm glad he didn't ask if I wanted him to come back with me; I would have said no, even though I really don't want to do this alone.

Once she gets my vitals and leads us into a room, she starts going over my family medical history before turning to Tom to ask him questions, too. He answers them in stride, apparently unbothered at sharing such invasive, personal information in front of me at short notice. Or, maybe he was just prepared for this to be part of the appointment.

I wish that I would have done more research on what was going to happen when I got here, but it's too late for that now. At least Tom's here with me.

Eventually, the nurse runs out of questions and stands, pulling a hospital gown from the cabinets behind her, handing them to me, and closing the curtains hanging around the examination table. I'll see the technician soon for the main event – the ultrasound.

"Nervous?" Tom asks, sounding way too calm for our situation; I start to think that maybe I'm the only one that grasps how serious this is.

"Yes," I say, giving him a wild look from behind the curtain because it should be obvious. "You're not?"

"More nervous than I've ever been in my life," he replies, and I guess if I look closely, I can see the pinched look on his face and the stiff set of his shoulders.

"Fooled me," I say, fitting the gown onto my body and pulling the curtain back. "Come stand up here; I don't want you looking up my vag."

"It's nothing I haven't seen before," he mutters, indulging my request.

"Oh, shut up," I say, laughing despite myself. "It's different right now."

"You don't think medical scenarios are hot?" he asks, quirking an eyebrow.

"Now is *not* the time," I giggle.

"So you *do*," he says gleefully.

He's only antagonizing me to take my mind off of my nerves, and I feel an odd mix of affection and irritation at his actions. I want him to take this seriously, but I think I need the silliness. He's winding up to say something else, but he's interrupted by a knock on the door.

"Michelle?" a young man with a kind voice asks, opening the door slightly to stick his head into the room. "Are you ready for me?"

"I am," I reply.

I'm not ready at all.

"Excellent," he says, smiling at me before glancing at Tom. "And this is Dad?"

"Tom's fine," he replies.

"I'm Paul," the technician says. "I know Carrie explained what was going to happen before I came in. Would you like me to go over that again?"

"Nope," I say, not in the mood to hear the entire process again. "I think I'm just ready to get into it."

"That eager, huh?" he asks, busying himself with setting up the equipment.

"Something like that," I mutter under my breath.

"I'm excited," Tom says, aggressively positive in a way that makes me want to kiss the air out of his lungs. "Nervous, too."

"That's normal for first-time parents," Paul replies, rolling a medical condom over the ultrasound wand. "Everything you're feeling is nothing that hasn't been felt before. It's to be expected, actually."

"That doesn't make me feel better," I say, watching as he positions himself at the end of the bed.

"It doesn't make anyone feel better," he laughs as he pulls the stirrups away from the exam table. "Do you mind putting your feet up here for me?"

"Yep," I say, transferring my weight to my elbows so I can slide into place. He instructs me to go further than I think is necessary, and it leaves me feeling completely exposed.

I block out most of what he's saying because of how overwhelmed I am with everything. I don't tune back into the conversation until the tech is sliding the wand inside of me. It isn't uncomfortable, but I'm very aware of the intrusion.

"Sorry if it's a little cold," he says, his eyes trained on the screen beside me.

Tom and I wait with bated breath as he looks for the baby, neither of us willing to say anything. The room isn't quiet long, though. There's a fast, whooshing sound that fills the space. I know what it is without Paul saying it.

"Is that…?" Tom trails off; his voice is cautious.

"The heartbeat?" the tech says, turning away from the screen. "It is. Now, if you look back here, you'll be able to see the outline of your little one."

It's nothing, really, just a little blob on the screen. Still, I'm bulldozed with a kind of love I've never felt before. I've not yet met my little one, but I know I'll do anything to protect them. I'll do whatever it takes to give my baby a good life.

"Wow," I breathe out, unable to look away from the little dot that's my child. "Wow."

"Yeah," Tom says, grabbing my hand. "Wow."

I lace our fingers together as the tech says a few more things and explains the measurements. Apparently, I'm about thirteen weeks along, and my due date is sometime in the middle of February. After snapping a picture, Paul takes the wand out of me, telling us he'll be right back with a copy we can take with us.

"How're you feeling?" Tom asks, leaning in close, his nose brushing against my hair as he nuzzles against me.

"I don't know," I answer honestly. Then, I pull my feet out of the stirrups and drop Tom's hand, not caring that my ass is out when I stand up. "Is 'everything' an appropriate answer?"

"Yeah," Tom laughs, getting up and closing the curtain around me. "That's exactly how I feel. Most of it's good, though."

"Almost all of it is good," I say as I slip out of the gown and back into my clothes.

I feel optimistic for the first time since finding out I'm pregnant. No matter what, it's this baby and me against the world. Especially while I'm growing them and carrying them with me everywhere, I'm even thinking that co-parenting won't be so bad. Tom's everything I'd want in the father of my child, and he's already so involved. Sure, things can change in an instant, but right now, things feel good; they feel right.

When Paul comes back with only one copy of the sonogram, I can see Tom's face fall out of the corner of my eye. I curse myself for not saying anything, but Tom doesn't either. I check with Paul to make sure we're all checked out before leading Tom out of the office.

"Here," I say when we get into his car, thrusting the envelope containing the picture of our baby toward him. "Take a picture of it. I'm sorry I didn't ask them to print another copy for you."

"It's okay," he says, his body seeming much lighter as he snaps a couple of photos. "I didn't think to ask, either."

He hands the envelope back to me before backing us out of the parking spot. I watch him, admiring his handsomeness and the smile that seems to be permanently etched onto his face. Something emboldens me and gives me the confidence to ask for more.

"Do you want to grab lunch?"

"I can't," he replies, sounding genuinely regretful. "I'm really tied up with some stuff at work. But, maybe we can do dinner sometime."

"Yeah," I say, trying my best to hide the fact that the rejection feels like a personal affront. "Sounds good."

Tom tries to talk to me the rest of the ride back to my apartment, but my head just isn't in it. Instead, I'm trying to use my logical brain to fend off the intense emotional reaction that's threatening to pull me down and into the undertow.

In front of my apartment, I think Tom is leaning in to kiss me, but I can't let him. Instead, I jump out of his car and gather my things from outside of the car.

"Thanks for driving me," I say, barely keeping my voice steady. "I hope the rest of your day goes well. Bye, Tom."

I step away, shutting the door even though Tom's still trying to talk to me. If I stay here, I'll start crying. It's these goddamn pregnancy hormones.

"I'll call you later," Tom yells out of his window before pulling away.

Somehow, I manage to keep the tears in until I'm in the sanctuary of my home. Then, I collapse onto the couch and cry, sobbing in ugly, loud gasps. There's nothing I can do to stop the onslaught of emotions. I hate it.

It's been happening more and more recently. I know it's because I'm growing another person, and my body isn't used to all the hormones coursing through it. I haven't looked to see when this pregnancy symptom goes away because I'm afraid of what my reaction may be if I find out that it doesn't. If I had to guess, I'd cry hysterically if I learn I have to deal with this for six more months.

Eventually, I manage to get the tears under control. Then, I clean my face up before FaceTime Pippa to show her the first picture of her niece or nephew.

CHAPTER 18
Tom

I'm still using work as a distraction, but it isn't as powerful of one anymore; it's hard to keep my mind off of Michelle's pregnancy when I'm working on an app that's aiming to become the number one place to find childcare in Houston. Everywhere I look, there's information for new parents and reminders that it's never too early to start thinking about your child's future.

It's been a long two weeks; most of my team has pivoted to other projects while Victor and I have taken on FamFirst. Once we get the bulk of the bug reports resolved, Victor's going to back off, and the app is going to become solely my responsibility.

Actually, it's mostly mine as-is. Victor's only helping because he's worried I bit off more than I can chew. Maybe I did in the first few days after the app was updated; there's no better beta testing than a product launch. FamFirst users flooded us with issues we missed in places we didn't even think to check.

Before I found out I'm going to be a dad, I might have welcomed this distraction; I still do a little, but only because I don't want to bother Michelle. Still, my mind is on her instead of work. Victor's assistance has made it even easier for me to zone out and think about how my and Michelle's lives are about to change.

I've been careful to keep our lives separate when I think about what's going to happen. Even though I want our futures to be woven together, I know the safest thing is to prepare for a life of co-parenting while I pine helplessly after Michelle. I wonder what our kid's going to be like. I wonder how Michelle will grow into motherhood. I wonder if she wants me there with her.

A Zoom call pops up on my laptop screen, stopping those dangerous thoughts from going any further. I'm a little confused as to why Ryan's calling me since we had a meeting this morning, but I answer it cheerfully. I know this is a business relationship, but he's becoming one of my favorite people to work with.

"Hey, Ryan," I say, turning on my camera when his face fills my entire screen. "Did we miss something during the meeting?"

"Nope," he replies. "But I have an answer to that glitch on the booking page you were talking about earlier."

"No shit?" I reply, grinning at the screen. "You some kind of code wizard now?"

"God no," he laughs, leaning forward to tap on his keyboard. "I just think it's the same as the glitch we ran into on the log-in page. I'll send it your way so you can look at it and tell me if I'm seeing things right."

The files appear in my inbox a few seconds later, just some screenshots of code, specifically the lines that were causing problems prior to launch. While I'm looking it over, I can tell Ryan's waiting with bated breath for my approval.

I'm pretty sure he's discovered an unknown passion in

coding. At first, his interest was purely professional – a check-in here and there to see how things were progressing. Then he started asking technical questions and was absolutely enthralled by the fact that things can be made or broken by something as small as a misplaced semicolon. So now he combs over lines of code just like we do.

"Well?" Ryan asks, unable to sit in the silence any longer.

"I think you're onto something here," I say after confirming he's correctly identified the issue. "What do you need us for?"

"You guys are experts," Ryan concedes, bristling with pride at my compliment. "There's no way I could pull any of this off."

"With time and practice, anything is possible," I say.

"Ain't that the truth?" he agrees. Then after a beat, he asks, "So, how's Michelle? Andrea says she hasn't been answering her texts."

"She's been busy," I say, checking to make sure my office door is closed. I'm dying to tell someone, and Ryan seems like a safe bet; he's so far away from us all. "Can you keep a secret?"

"A secret?" he asks, scooting closer to his screen. "What kind of secret?"

"Can you keep a secret?" I ask again, feeling giddy because I'm *finally* going to tell someone – provided Ryan promises he's not going to go blabbing to Andrea. "Like, just between us?"

"Yeah, man," he says, his features getting serious. "Between us."

"Michelle's pregnant," I blurt, unable to keep the massive grin from forming on my face.

Ryan blinks at the screen like he doesn't quite understand

what I'm saying. But then, the confusion is gone and replaced with genuine happiness and excitement.

"That's incredible!" he says, his voice a faux-whisper; I realize I probably should have asked if there were others around him since the FamFirst office is an open-air kind of thing, but it's too late for that now. "Congratulations, man. I'm happy for you."

"Thanks, Ryan," I say, my cheeks hurting with how hard I'm smiling. "Not many people know yet, though, so–"

"Between us," he replies. "I get it. When we found out Andrea was pregnant, we weren't going to tell anyone but her family until after we knew if we were having a little boy or a little girl. I let it slip to one of our investors before then because I was so excited. I get it."

"Thanks," I laugh, glad I have someone who gets it.

"So, how far along is she?"

"About fifteen weeks," I say, trying to remember everything from the obstetrician's appointment. "I think. I was with her at the appointment, but I didn't really hear much. I was too busy looking at the ultrasound screen."

"You got a picture?" Ryan asks, apparently sensing my eagerness to show off the sonogram.

"Yeah," I say, scrambling to get my phone out of my pocket. I triple-check to make sure the recipient is actually Ryan and not someone else before firing it off. "I just sent it."

"Would you look at that," he says, smiling down at his own phone. I know it's completely for my benefit, that there's nothing uniquely special about the black and white picture of a little blob, but still, he seems genuinely excited for me. "How're you feeling about it?"

"Nervous as hell," I admit, knowing he'll understand where I'm coming from. "But I'm excited."

"And how's Michelle?"

I wish I had an answer for him. Actually, it would be nice if I were able to come clean about everything and get his advice, but I've taken that lie too far, and there's no way I can tell Ryan.

"She's doing about the same," I say, opting for what feels like a safe response. "We weren't really planning on a baby."

"I felt similarly, and we *were* planning on having a baby. So I can't imagine being blindsided by it," he laughs. "It makes a lot of sense why you guys stopped coming out with everyone, though. I figured you were just avoiding us."

"God no," I reply, chuckling at how quickly Ryan connected the dots. "We missed y'all, but Michelle didn't want to explain why she wasn't drinking."

"I hear you loud and clear," Ryan says, glancing at something offscreen. "I'm sorry; I don't mean to cut this conversation short, but I've gotta get off of here. Let me know when you guys announce this officially. I know Andrea'll want to talk to Michelle all about it."

"I'll mention letting Andrea know," I say, even though I won't. Michelle's probably ready to be done with this little act we've been putting on.

"She'd appreciate that," he replies. "I'll talk to you soon, Tom."

"See ya, Ryan."

The call ends, and I pivot back to work. While I'm fixing the issue Ryan spotted, I let my mind wander to what it would be like if we were actually married and living the life Ryan and Andrea think we're living. I wonder if Michelle would want to make a grand announcement or keep the news to ourselves.

I haven't told anyone yet, even though I know my mom would be beside herself with excitement. It's no secret that she wants a grandchild; she's been asking my sister when she and her boyfriend are going to settle down and have a baby since he started coming to family holidays. Sure, she'll be disappointed that I'm having a child out of wedlock, but she's an open-minded woman. She'd come around if it means she gets to be a grandma.

Michelle and I haven't talked much about our next steps. It's not for lack of trying on either of our parts. If she's free, I'm working; if I'm free, she's working. At this point, we need to schedule a time and make ourselves available.

I don't want it to be something serious and formal, though. I care about her as more than just the mother of my child. The feelings I was starting to harbor for her are still here and are growing even stronger. I've never stopped wanting to pursue a romantic relationship with her.

It's on me to make that clear, though. Michelle has so much on her plate; dating is probably the last thing on her mind. However, I'm not opposed to taking charge here; after I confirm that what I've done has fixed the glitch, I text Michelle asking if she has time for a phone call. I'll be damned if I ask her on a real date over text.

My phone rings about twenty minutes later, Michelle's name is on the screen. I let it ring for a few seconds, so I don't seem overeager before answering.

"Hey. I wasn't expecting you to be available so soon," I say, aiming for a casual tone.

"It's nice to hear from you, too," she says sarcastically but not unkindly. "It's my day off."

"I won't take up too much of your time then," I promise.

"It's not like I'm doing anything else," she quips."What's up?"

"Well," I begin, a little nervous now that I'm actually

doing this, "I was thinking about how good of a team we made when we were pretending to be a couple."

"You were?" she asks, a hint of apprehension on her tongue.

"I was," I confirm. "And I got to thinking... what if we tried it for real?"

Michelle is quiet, and I can't tell if it's a good kind of quiet or not. It makes me nervous, so I keep talking.

"I just had a lot of fun being your fake husband," I say. Then, when I realize that makes it worse, I add, "Not that I think we should go that fast or anything. I just thought it might be nice to take you out on a real date."

"I see," Michelle says. She sounds hesitant, but more like she can't doesn't fully believe this is happening.

"I know weekends aren't good for you because of your job at Metro," I say, pushing through because I have a good feeling about this. "So I was wondering if you'd be willing to accompany me on a date this Tuesday at, say, seven?"

"Wednesday would work better for me," she says, and I can hear the beginnings of a smile in her voice.

"Wednesday works great for me. I'll pick you up at your place?" I ask, trying to reign in my excitement, at least for the duration of this conversation.

"Yeah," she replies, sounding a lot like I feel. "Yeah, that sounds great."

"Awesome. I, uh, I have to get back to work, but I'll talk to you soon."

"Bye, Tom," she says, her voice warm and genuine and full of affection.

After we hang up, I sit and stare at my computer screen, processing what just happened. When I convince myself that, yes, that was real, I give into the urge to fist-bump the air.

Eddy sees me through the glass wall of my office, and as I come back into myself, I realize he's staring.

He raises his eyebrow and cocks his head in a way that asks, "*What happened?*"

I stand from my desk and yank the door open to announce to the entire office, "I have a date with Michelle! A real one!"

CHAPTER 19
Michelle

I'm trying not to freak out. Tom has pulled out all the stops tonight, and I don't trust that this is all because he likes *me*. I've been waiting for him to bring up the baby, but he hasn't. Instead, this has been all about getting to know me.

Well, until our food got to the table. Tom's eating a steak, the most expensive one on the menu, cooked to a perfect shade of deep pink. I opted for a chicken dish, even though I would have preferred the halibut; maybe if things between us go well, we can come back here when I'm not pregnant, and I can order all the things I want but can't have.

Our server has cleared away our empty entree plates and dropped off refills of our mocktails (Tom isn't drinking in solidarity), and now we're waiting for the peanut butter and jelly cake she recommended to arrive.

"I'm going to be honest," Tom says, his tongue darting out from between his lips to catch stray droplets of his beverage, "I don't know if I'm going to be able to eat more than one bite of that cake."

"Me either," I laugh.

"She really talked me into that one," he admits. "I wouldn't have ordered that on my own."

"I wouldn't have before I got pregnant, but I was actually thinking about it before she suggested it," I say, offering the first piece of information pertaining to the baby since we got here. "I've been having the weirdest cravings."

"Like what?" he asks softly like he's afraid to pry too far. He's watching me with rapt attention; I almost forget to breathe.

"Some standard stuff like peanut butter and pickles," I say, feeling like sharing this is more important than sharing the story of how my dad left us. "But lately, I've been craving *chalk*."

"No!" he says, sounding scandalized. "That can't be a good sign."

"It's actually super common," I say, laughing at his dumbfounded expression. "It's a sign of low iron. I'm on prenatals now, so hopefully, those cravings stop."

He's saved from coming up with an answer when our dessert is dropped at the table. Before the server walks away, he finds his voice and asks for a box to go. Our conversation dies down to something a little less intimate to keep from being interrupted.

We joke about the weirdest things we've eaten. For me, it was a bowl of oatmeal I mixed crunchy peanut butter and an ungodly amount of brown sugar and honey into; for Tom, it was a hotdog dressed with Honey Nut Cheerios and chocolate syrup. Then, after our food is boxed up and our check is paid, Tom stands and offers me his hand. I take it and let him lead me to the valet station.

When we get into his car, I realize I'm not ready for this date to be over yet. One glance at the speedometer confirms we're going below the speed limit; Tom doesn't want this to be over either. I'm trying to figure out a way to extend this, but he beats me to the punch.

"Sorry if this is too forward, but what do you think about going back to my place?"

"I'd like that," I reply, feeling like a teenager getting swept up in the throes of her first crush. A grin spreads over my face; in the driver's seat, I can tell Tom's feeling a similar sense of excitement.

He drives us a little outside of town to Hyde Park. He's apologetic about the drive, but I don't mind. It means we get to spend more time together. We talk about nothing, but the sexual tension is building in the air – we both know what the invitation back to his house means.

We pull into his driveway, and he instructs me to stay put. I watch as he crosses in front of the hood of the car. Then, he opens my door and offers me his hand. I take it and let him help me to my feet and up the path to the front entrance.

Tom's house is modest, considering how much money he makes. It's a single-story brick home with a large porch outfitted with hand-made wooden deck furniture. The landscaping is decent but lacks a personal touch – too many hedges and not enough flowers. I wonder if he'd be open to suggestions because I can already think of a couple off the top of my head.

"Sorry about the mess," he says as he leads me into the entryway. "I wasn't planning on having company."

"I wasn't expecting to come back," I reply, not seeing the mess he's apologizing for. "I'm not that kind of girl."

"Of course not," he laughs, leading me through the house. "You want anything to drink? I'm not a master mixologist or anything, but I could probably come up with a mean mocktail if you give me a few minutes."

"No, I'm all right," I say. Then, when we slow down in the living room, I add, "I want to see your bedroom, though."

He stops to look at me curiously as he makes sense of what I've just said. Then, when it clicks, he grabs my hand and pulls me through the house with a youthful bounce in his step. I wish we weren't going so fast; Tom's eye for interior design is better than his taste for landscaping.

Once I'm pulled past the threshold of his bedroom, I can no longer observe my surroundings, not that I want to; he pulls me against him to kiss the wind out of my lungs without bothering to close the door.

I respond as best I can, but Tom's relentless, working his tongue into my mouth and licking against my teeth. The noises that escape my mouth are involuntary; I'm so inundated with his taste, smell, and touch.

"Go lie down for me," he says, his voice husky; I can't help but obey.

As I'm settling onto the mattress, the lights come on.

"I want to see you," he says by way of explanation. "Is that okay?"

"More than okay," I say, a jolt of arousal ricocheting through my body at the idea of being so desired.

"Good," he says, coming to the bed and dropping to his elbows to lean over me.

My breath catches in my throat as I wait for him to connect our lips again. This time, he connects our mouths softly in a gentle, exploratory gesture. As we kiss, his body melts into mine – his chest, then his abdomen, then his hips. He's already half-hard and making no attempts to hide it.

I grind up into him, relishing the way his cock continues to harden against me. He's restraining himself, resisting the urge to grind into me; it's evident in the slight twitch of his hips and the quivering of his arms on either side of my head.

Unexpectedly, Tom pulls away, sliding down the length of my body. I prop myself on my elbows to watch him slide off my kitten heel. Then, he presses a kiss to the sole of each of my feet before making his way up the inside of my calves. He mouths at the side of my knee, then nips at the sensitive skin of my inner thighs.

His hands slide up my outer thighs and under my dress to the waistband of my panties. I suck in a harsh breath when he pulls them down, exposing my dripping pussy to the air. Much to my dismay, he doesn't immediately give me attention where I'm aching for it.

I'm not left completely disappointed, though. He works his way slowly up to my mouth, kissing my body through my dress. A shiver runs through my body when he drags his tongue along the column of my neck.

"I told you I wanted to take my time with you," Tom whispers in my ear, causing goosebumps to bloom down my arm. "I intend to do that."

Then he resumes ravishing me by capturing my lips with his, one hand cupping my cheek as the other starts pushing my dress past my hips to my belly button. He pulls away, stroking his thumb along my jaw before taking my clothes off completely, lifting me off the bed just enough to yank the garment over my head.

"Not wearing a bra?" he asks, looking from my full breasts to my face.

"Didn't think I needed one," I challenge.

"You don't," Tom replies. "You're perfect."

The praise washes over me, swirling in the air around us as I inhale it into my lungs. He returns his mouth to my chest, kissing at the supple flesh before moving to my nipple. He sucks at the hardened peak, drawing a moan from my throat.

When I'm squirming below him, and he's satisfied with the reactions he's drawn from me, Tom moves on to the other.

"I could listen to the sounds you make for the rest of my life," he drawls, kissing between my breasts before moving to my stomach. "Like music to my ears."

I try to speak, but nothing coherent comes out. My brain short-circuits as his tongue swirls around my navel. He lingers there for a moment before giving attention to the rest of my stomach. I'm not showing much; I look more bloated than I do pregnant, but Tom adores me all the same.

"God, you're beautiful like this," he says against my skin. "Look at you. So gone on the pleasure you can't even talk. You want my tongue, sweetheart?"

"Your cock," I manage to say. "Please."

"Well, since you asked so nicely," he replies, shifting so he's no longer trapped between my thighs.

He undresses quickly with no decorum, flinging his shirt and tie to one side of the bed and his pants and boxers to the other. I have no time to admire his cock before he's hovering over me again, his tip resting against the folds of my cunt.

"Are you ready for me, baby?" he asks, mouthing at my neck as he speaks. "Ready for my cock?"

"I'm ready for your cock, Tom," I whine. "*Please* fuck m–"

The rest of my sentence is cut off by Tom thrusting into me in a quick motion. He doesn't give me any time to adjust to his length, pounding into me relentlessly. My fake nails dig into his back as I try to anchor myself, drawing a growl out of him. He bites down on my shoulder, and I cry out as my orgasm builds rapidly.

His headboard starts to bang against the wall as his rhythm speeds up. I try to reign in my inarticulate babbling.

Finally, I manage to grunt out his name to beg him for more, but I only get a warm chuckle in return.

"What is it, Michelle?" he asks, the sound of my name on his lips carving into my chest like a hot knife. "Tell me what you want."

I can't, not with the pace at which he's driving his rock-hard length into my G-spot. After a few minutes of trying to tell him I'm close, he finally realizes *he's* rendering me speechless and slows his movements down.

"Go ahead," he says. "Tell me what you want."

I don't know what possesses me to say it – maybe it's the baby hormones, maybe it's because I just want Tom more than I've wanted any other person before – but I blurt, "I want you to get me pregnant again."

That seems to awaken something primal in him because he starts fucking me with renewed vigor. The sharp sound of skin slapping against skin fills the room as he buries his face into my neck, pressing open-mouthed kisses that are more teeth than lips along my flesh.

Tom says, "That's it; I'll get you pregnant again if that's what you want. Anything for my baby."

Then he groans, and the movement of his hips stutters as he comes inside me, filling me up and getting me irritatingly close to the edge. He's nearly turned into a deadweight on top of me as he's taken by pleasure.

That's not a problem, though. I take matters into my own hands, literally, but reaching down between the two of us to touch myself. It doesn't take much; the combined pressure of Tom's cock still hard inside me and my own steady attention to my clit is all I need to follow him over the edge.

My body tightens around him, and for a few seconds, we're one being. He pulls out when he starts to soften, but he stays over me to catch his breath. Eventually, something about our position strikes me as funny, and giggles bubble out of me. They're contagious, and soon Tom is laughing into my hair.

"That was incredible," I say.

At the same time, he says, "Will you be my girlfriend?"

"What?" I ask, still chuckling when I push him away from my chest to see him properly. It's not that I didn't hear him, but because I want to hear him ask again.

"I asked if you would be my girlfriend," he says, grinning at me, "You know, like officially."

"Yes," I answer breathlessly. "I'd love to be your girlfriend."

"Yeah," he asks, scanning my face.

"Yeah," I reply, sinking into the kiss he gives me in response. And, when he starts to get hard again, I let my hands roam to his body for another round.

Epilogue
TOM

5 MONTHS LATER

"Hey, hey!" I say, dropping the box in my hands and rushing to the front door to grab the overflowing shopping bag of my old textbooks from Michelle's hands. "What are you doing?"

"I'm trying to help," she says stubbornly, stepping back so her baby bump doesn't knock into the tote.

"No offense, sweetheart, but you're about to pop," I laugh. "If you want to help, maybe you can unpack the linens?"

Michelle rolls her eyes, something she's taken to doing more the closer we get to her due date. It's because she hates that she isn't able to do *everything* she wants to do. I know that leaving most of the details of the move up to me has been killing her, too. Unfortunately for her, it's a hell of a lot easier moving before the baby gets here rather than after.

"I'll just watch you," she says.

"See something you like?" I ask playfully, leading her through the house. *Our* house.

"Yeah," she replies. "All this heavy lifting is doing wonders for your arms... and your ass."

"Are you sure you can't go hang out with Pippa?" I ask, my face heating up.

"She's working," Michelle says, sighing dramatically as she drops herself onto the white sectional our movers dropped off two days ago. "But I think she's coming over later."

"Ah, did she say that?"

"No," she replies conversationally. "But I can feel it in my bones."

"I should have known moving to Houston meant I was going to have to fight with her for your attention," I laugh.

"Tom," she whines dramatically. "I sleep in your bed every night."

"For now," I tease, dropping the tote in front of the bookcase we've yet to put together. "I remain unconvinced you aren't going to move into your bedroom at her place."

"Even if I do, you're the one I'm in love with."

"I'm hoping that's enough," I say.

I don't doubt her love for me. However, she was slow to admit it, almost like she was afraid I wouldn't feel the same or that I'd use her feelings against her. Convincing her that I'm not her dad has been an ongoing endeavor, but I don't mind. The way she's opened up to me is worth it.

"You're more than enough," she replies, waddling over to me. "You know that."

"I guess I do," I reply, grabbing her face and leaning over to kiss her.

"I want to get married," Michelle tells me when we part.

I stare down at her, looking for some sort of indication

that she's messing with me. Then, when I don't find any, I ask, "Are you serious?"

"As a heart attack," she confirms.

"Is this a marriage proposal?"

"No," Michelle says. "It's just me letting you know that I'm ready when you are."

I chuckle, cup the base of her skull in my hands, and press a lingering kiss to her forehead. She sways into me, pressing her stomach into mine. I let my fingertips travel down her arms to the bump.

"I think Ben's sleeping," she says.

I smirk at her and bend down to talk directly to the baby. "It's okay if you're napping, Evelyn."

We decided to keep the baby's gender a surprise. It's made shopping for the nursery a little difficult – most of the decor we've come across has been gendered. Michelle made the call to decorate the nursery with all the colors of the rainbow, and it turned out perfect. It only took her four months of shopping to put it all together.

"It's a boy," she says, grabbing onto one of my hands and moving it so I can feel the baby's body. "I can tell."

"Sure you can," I reply, still in awe of the way I can feel our little one. "We're just going to have to wait and see who's right."

Truthfully, I don't care either way. I'm beyond excited for them to get here. Michelle is, too, but she's more tired of being pregnant than anything else.

"I guess we are," she says warmly, stepping away from me. "I'll be right back. I have to pee."

"Hold on. I don't think there's toilet paper in the bathroom," I reply, walking past her. "There's some in my car."

"Just meet me there," she says. "I'm not going to wait."

"Fine," I laugh, breaking into a jog so she doesn't have to

wait on me too long. I'm back in the house in less than thirty seconds.

"Thanks," she says, taking the roll from my hand before pushing me out. I grab the door and pull it closed to give her some privacy.

I head back to my car to grab the rest of the bathroom stuff. While I'm digging through the backseat to see if there are any other essentials we might have missed, my phone vibrates in my back pocket – a message from Ryan.

There's been a change in the board of directors at FamFirst; the company started to grow rapidly with the updated interface. A popular family influencer shared a video about how awesome her nanny is and mentioned that she uses FamFirst for childcare. Usage in Houston exploded, and there was an influx of inquiries about expanding to other cities.

It didn't make sense to outsource the work anymore – my guys were getting overloaded, and it was starting to get pricey. So, I sold my share of the agency and my house to be the head of software development for FamFirst. Not only is the pay better, but I'll be spending a lot less time at work, which means I can focus on Michelle and our baby.

About a month after Michelle and I started officially dating, we made the decision to let Ryan and Andrea know we weren't entirely truthful when we first met. Of course, they don't need to know that we weren't together when we first met. Sometimes white lies between friends are good.

I'm expecting the message to be about our move, but instead, he's asking me if I can keep a secret, just between the two of us. I throw a glance toward the front of our farmhouse before I tell him that, yes, I can keep a secret.

My phone starts ringing less than a minute after the message goes through, and Ryan tells me in one breath that Andrea's pregnant, even though they weren't trying.

Printed in Great Britain
by Amazon